PIRATE GOLD

ORDER OF THE BLACK SUN - BOOK 27

PRESTON WILLIAM CHILD

PROLOGUE

"Why have you boarded us, captain?"

"Admiral," Walton Ogden corrected. If he was going to be addressed by his title, he always preferred that it be the correct one. "A captain commands one vessel. I command many."

The captain of this captured ship rolled his eyes and wiped some blood off his face. He was probably just annoyed with himself. He had been such easy prey for Admiral Walton Ogden and his pirate crew. He hadn't put up much of a fight and now they were going to rob him dry, striping the defeated vessel clean of any and all things valuable.

It had become almost routine for Admiral Ogden. It was hardly even a challenge at all anymore. Though, it was made all the more easy that he had more than a dozen pirate ships at his command. He used to use them all for one score and completely overwhelm the target with superior numbers. That was when they were all less experienced. Now he could take a ship with his own ship rather easily, and his fleet would disperse and each part of it would do the same. Every three months they would gather and pool their spoils together.

Admiral Ogden had become one the most feared names on the seas, and his pirate fleet caused just as much panic. No one dared challenge him; not with that many fighters and that many cannons under his command.

As much as he enjoyed leading so many vessels, he was happy he could do it from the security of his flagship, the *Scarlet Wing*. Under its dark red sails, he always felt easy no matter what he was doing, even if he was running his sword through someone's stomach.

"Why do you think I've boarded you?" Admiral Ogden asked the captain of the shipping vessel they were standing on. Ogden's crew were already running around the ship, taking whatever they could find. The defeated sailors on board had no choice except to comply or die at this point. "To have a drink? Or perhaps I just wished to speak to such a legendary and esteemed captain of shipping frigate like you ... the notorious ... what was your name?" Before the captain could answer, Ogden continued. "Oh, that's right, I don't care because you are nobody. What the hell do you think I'm doing here?"

"You're pillaging us," the captain said.

"Precisely. You tried to fight us off. You failed of course, so now we are going to claim our reward for our efforts."

The honest truth was that this shipping vessel probably wouldn't give Admiral Ogden and his fleet much, but the crew had been itching for a fight. Hopefully this was enough to satisfy them until they moved on to their next target. Until they could find something with a prize that was really worth fighting and dying over.

"You said you command many ships," the shipping captain said uneasily. "You are him, aren't you? Ogden. The pirate admiral."

"That's me, yes," Ogden smirked.

"You and that damned armada of devils haven't gotten enough yet? You just have to keep attacking innocent people—"

"No one in the world is innocent, my friend."

The shipping captain spat on the deck and started yelling. "When will it be enough? How much do you need? How much more?"

Admiral Ogden considered the question, and he pondered it still for some time after. One day, long after he and his crew had raided that shipping vessel, he finally realized the answer to that question.

No amount of gold would ever be enough to satisfy him.

1

BROKE AND BROKEN

Life was much harder without money—and David Purdue hated it. It hadn't been long since he was able to purchase almost everything he ever wanted. The things he couldn't buy, he still managed to get thanks to the resources he could afford. If he wanted to go across the world, he'd just use his private jet. Now he could barely manage to get down the street by anything other than his own two feet.

There weren't many billionaires in the world and even less former billionaires. The few who had that much money didn't often lose it. How was it even possible to lose that much money? It was an absurd thought to even consider.

David Purdue, though, was a former billionaire. He'd lost it all—no—it was taken from him.

One of the most dangerous enemies he'd ever made over

his many years of trotting the globe had literally returned from death to haunt him, and to take everything from him.

Julian Corvus and his secret society, the Order of the Black Sun, had robbed Purdue blind. They'd taken anything he had any connection to. They hacked into his finances and drained all of his accounts. They burned his house to the ground. They stole all of the artifacts that he had spent years collecting and protecting. They had even taken his friends prisoner.

To top it off, Julian and the Black Sun tried to kill him. They left him to die in the inferno that they turned his house into. He would have burned too, if one of their own members hadn't seen just how dangerous Julian Corvus was. She had pulled Purdue out of that fire, because she thought he was the only one who could stop the Black Sun.

Maybe he was...but it didn't seem likely anymore.

As far as most of the world knew—and as far as that order of maniacs knew—David Purdue was dead. He died inside of his burning home. His fabled collection of artifacts was nowhere to be found in the scorched remains of his estate. It seemed that the exceptionally rich man had ended up having an exceptionally painful death.

Some days, he felt like he might as well be dead. He was left with nothing. Homeless, broke, and alone, he spent every day wandering around just trying to survive. The little cash he managed to scavenge was used on food or water, anything just to keep breathing.

Shortly before he lost it all, a psychic woman had warned him about his impending defeat and everything she said came true. So hopefully, her final words of foresight to him would come true as well.

"The only one who can lay a dead man to rest is another dead man."

Julian Corvus was the dead man who came and ruined him, revived by an ancient spear blessed with some unknown power. Now Purdue was, for all intents and purposes, dead. So, if those predictions were as accurate as they seemed, maybe he had a chance of making sure Julian stayed dead this time.

With his current conditions, though, there was no way of even attempting to stand up to Julian. He had nothing to use against him. He had no way of getting to him. If he tried anything now, he'd be killed immediately. The Black Sun would be finishing the job that they thought they started back when they tried to kill him.

The people who tried to murder him, who thought they had, almost gave him an advantage in a strange way. Now he could catch them off guard, just like how they had ambushed him.

Purdue wanted to reclaim everything that was his. He wanted that more than he wanted anything, but it wouldn't be an easy task. It would be nearly impossible. He at least needed some sort of money just to get himself balanced again. Just having a roof over his head would be a good place to start.

Back when he was rich, Purdue had spent so much time gallivanting all over the world in his private jet on exotic expeditions to faraway places, he had never known how terrifying a normal everyday street could be. He never knew the worry of not being able to get food or shelter. He had never known what it was like to have no comforts at all. Even in his most stressful and dangerous of times before, he could always afford at least a small comfort or advantage. Now, he was a completely different person.

And he hated every second of being poor.

There was one way to get a small portion of his billions back. It wouldn't come close to replenishing his lost fortune entirely but it would at least be a start, and would still be an incredible amount of money by normal standards.

However, it was a long shot. It probably wasn't even worth the trouble it would take ... then again, if it meant helping him get back everything that was taken, then it maybe it was worth it after all. There was only one way to know for sure.

Purdue remembered the story of Admiral Walton Ogden's pirate fleet and the unbelievable amount of ships that fleet had plundered, and the absurd amount of treasure they had taken. He'd known that swashbuckling piece of history for years but had never given it more than a passing thought. It was interesting on its own, but compared to the things he'd learned about in all of his travels, it wasn't more remarkable than most of those, at least on the surface.

Only recently, when he had visited the New England Pirate Museum in Salem during his last artifact hunt, was Purdue reminded of that story, and the thought occurred to him that finding the pirate fleet's treasure might be something worth looking into. Now, it was more than just an interesting notion—it was a necessity.

Admiral Ogden and his pirate fleet had supposedly amassed a mountain of gold from hundreds of raids and battles. No one knew where the treasure trove was, despite many having tried finding it to no success. They were mostly just searching the seas blindly, apparently hoping to just stumble upon the gargantuan amount of treasure. Many tried, and they had all failed miserably at finding anything.

Everyone who tried finding it lacked a key tool for any search—a map. The blueprints they would need make their way to the treasure, to all of the riches an entire armada of criminals had claimed from their enemies.

Purdue didn't share the problem that anyone who had tried before had. The map that they needed was not some hypothetical, unattainable thing. He already owned it. He had for years. Purdue bought the map at an auction for a few millions on a whim, back when that kind of money was nothing more than pocket change for him. Unlike most of the old relics he collected, Admiral Ogden's map hadn't been part of the collection that the Order of the Black Sun absconded with.

The treasure map hadn't been displayed with the rest. He preferred that his collection be solely rare items with a variety of values, uses, and insight to different cultures of old. A map leading to a pile of pirate gold wasn't overly exciting to a man who already had far more money than almost any amount of gold would be worth.

Now, with all of his circumstances having changed, that lost gold suddenly became far more enticing than it had been before. He needed money desperately, and maybe finding Admiral Ogden's treasure hoard was the best way to get himself back on track. Once he had some funds, he could start planning how to get his friends back, his property back, and his life back.

Admiral Ogden's treasure could be the key.

The map wasn't with his collection but was hopefully still where he left it; in a safety deposit box at one of his banks. He hadn't dared go inside since the Order of the Black Sun attacked and drained all of his accounts. They though he was dead and he wanted to keep it that way. Going to a public place where he could easily be identified wasn't a smart move.

Having spent weeks on the streets, half-starved and unkempt, he hardly looked like the late billionaire David Purdue at all. Rather, he was a peasant in comparison, a beggar who would have never even been looked at by the man he used to be. David Purdue would never have taken notice of someone like him, and certainly could have never imagined becoming that way.

If he could barely recognize himself, then it was likely that others would have trouble too.

Purdue crossed the street to the bank. Most people who passed him ignored him completely. Others glanced at him with revulsion at his smell.

All he could do was hope that the contents of his deposit box hadn't been removed just yet. If the bank got notice of his death and then purged his box, then there went his contingency plan.

He went into the lobby, which was empty on a mid-week afternoon, and approached one of the tellers. She gave him a pleasant smile but he could see the displeasure on her face. He looked worse for wear and he most assuredly reeked. He looked far different than most of the richer clientele this bank did business with, than the kind of customer he used to be. Still, the teller kept up the professional pretenses well enough.

"Good morning," she said with that forced smile still unnaturally stretched across her face. "How can I help you today?"

He tried to return her smile but in his current state, he probably looked like a skunk bearing its teeth. She squirmed in response to his pitiful attempt at friendliness and he could tell she was avoiding breathing through her nose.

"Aye," Purdue said. "I would like to access my safe deposit box."

She looked at him uncertainly, straining to recognize him, probably thinking it was impossible that someone like him was actually an established customer. Finally, she turned to her computer monitor.

"Your name?"

He didn't want to say it out loud. That name belonged to someone who was supposed to be burnt to crisp. For all he knew, the Order of the Black Sun made sure that the name alone would trigger all sorts of alarms. He wouldn't put it past them, especially with a psychopath like Julian Corvus now leading them. He couldn't risk it.

"I have the box number, if that helps."

"I would need the name as well," she said firmly. "For security. If you have some sort of identification..."

He used to have identification but those cards were just more kindling for the fire that burned through his house. He had nothing to use anymore. Not that it mattered, really. The Black Sun had erased him from most places. He probably wasn't even in the bank's systems anymore either.

"Sorry, I don't," Purdue said with a sigh, poking around his pockets just for emphasis. "But if I could just get a peek at the box, eh? Just this once."

"I'm sorry, sir, but I can't do that." She didn't look very

sorry. If anything, she looked relieved to not have to help him.

"Not to worry," Purdue said with fake innocence. "I am sure things will sort themselves out."

This wasn't unexpected. He always doubted he'd be able to just stroll in and retrieve the contents of his safe deposit box. It was a hope, since it was the easiest option. He didn't want to go to his backup plan, but in this case, there wasn't another choice.

His lack of any and all resources—including even his own name—had left him with very few options.

Purdue could try his hand at slipping a robbery note, but that would undoubtedly end in complete and utter failure. Even if he miraculously pulled it off, that would put far too many eyes on him. He would have the attention of the law, and probably the Order of the Black Sun. If the police didn't find him, Julian Corvus and his secret society certainly would, and they would finish what they started this time. They would be certain that Purdue was really dead.

No.

He had to be smarter than that. He had very few tools at his disposal. His charm was usually one of his more useful attributes, but his current appearance dampened its appeal. Besides that, his only remaining possession was an old journal—a book of shadows that had been written by a psychotic, old witch centuries ago. It had been the latest addition to his collection, and now was the sole remaining artifact he owned. It was filled with disturbing experiments and gruesome spells. Its author, Mona Greed, had been the most wicked of real witches.

After acquiring it, and seeing the terrible things inside, he had wanted nothing more than to burn it, but it was impossible to burn thanks to a protection its author had placed on it. So, he wanted to bury it where no one could ever find it.

Now, though, he found himself sometimes relieves that he still had it. As awful as the book was, it was better than having nothing. He considered selling it to some occult store or to some practicing witches. The journal was practically legendary among the witch community, but he didn't want to spread the vile writing inside. It was too dangerous to give to someone else.

Even if he might be able to fetch a decent price for the book of shadows, it was hardly enough to start rebuilding his life. He could always sell the wretched thing after he found Admiral Ogden's treasure; when it was no longer his only asset and it wasn't the only thing that he could still call his own.

While Purdue wasn't any kind of witch or wizard, the old spell book had knowledge that could be used in other ways.

Feeling beaten after his visit to the bank, Purdue sat on a bench and flipped through the old book of shadows. Just as he did, every time he opened the book, he would do his best not to linger on any page too long. He didn't want to see more of that witch's disturbing musings than he needed to. There were things in there ... things too dark to let the mind think about. There were instructions inside to perform all sorts of cruel acts with magic.

With the spells inside, he could set the whole bank on fire in an instant or have everyone working there spontaneously combust, but he didn't want or need anything so violent.

Luckily, the book of shadows also contained a recipe for something of a sleeping powder. Perfect for someone like him, who wasn't a sadistic lunatic wanting to torture people with magic. The ingredients were all natural and easy enough to find. They were just used in a combination that most people would never think of. Once they were mixed together, he just had to say a few words from the book and the powder would be ready for use.

Purdue never thought he would ever become a bank robber, but life threw curve balls sometimes. He just had to adapt to the unforeseen twists and turns that kept coming his way; which was easier ever since the biggest twist of all had happened. Everything seemed possible now that everything he owned had been taken right under his nose.

Besides, it would hardly be considered a robbery at all. It wasn't one. Not really. He was just taking back his own belongings. No one was going to be robbed, and nothing was going to be stolen from someone.

It was more of a complicated withdrawal than it was a robbery.

Still, whatever he considered, he had to be careful in its handling. If he didn't play things right, his face would end up on the evening news and the entire country would be out looking for him. He couldn't risk that.

INTERLUDE 1 – SAM CHECKS IN EVERY DAY

Sam Cleave never stayed in one motel for more than a day. That was the safest decision he could make given the life-threatening circumstances he now found himself in. That call from Purdue had really shaken him to the core, but he knew better than to doubt Purdue ... especially after he heard what happened next.

That one phone call of warning was enough for him to upend his life and take off. According to Purdue at the time, the Order of the Black Sun was coming after him, with Julian Corvus leading them. Sam had watched Julian die back in Norwich ... but he knew better than to doubt anything these days. There were no rules when it came to the artifacts they were all fighting for. It was entirely possible that psycho had Julian survived, or was somehow brought back from death.

Purdue had warned him that the Black Sun would probably be coming after Sam too. That made sense. Julian seemed like the type of leader who would stress thoroughness in getting rid of the ancient order's enemies. So, that made Sam near the top of the Black Sun's most wanted list. After all, he'd help Purdue take that secret society down a number of times.

It had all been so fast, and so cryptic, but right away he packed all of the essentials and took off, and hadn't stopped running since. Purdue's warning was scary enough, but the scarier part was seeing the news the next day—that billionaire David Purdue had died in a house fire at his estate. If those bastards really had managed to kill Purdue, Sam knew they wouldn't hesitate doing the same to him. He hoped their other frequent colleague, Nina Gould, was alright but he doubted it. Purdue said she hadn't picked up his call. Maybe she didn't get the warning like Sam had.

He tried to at least count himself lucky. If Purdue really was dead, he was thankful that his friend had managed to give him a fighting chance, or at least a head start in staying alive. Sam tried to mourn Purdue in his own way after he heard the news. The two of them had shared some friction here and there throughout working together, but overall, he was always thankful to have known that spoiled, entitled, bastard.

Sam had always been pretty adaptable to whatever curve balls life threw at him and he treated this no differently. It was just another investigation, another job. The only difference was this time, the story he was fighting so hard for was his own survival.

The motel he was currently at was seedy, to say the least, but he was okay with it. The more rundown and inconspicuous the better. As expansive as the Black Sun was, and how good they were at finding things, they couldn't check every dusty old building on the planet. There were plenty of places to hide, and so far he was doing a good job staying out of their sights. He hoped to keep it that way.

He lay in a rickety bed, staring up at the ceiling and—just like he did every day—tried to think of how he was going to get out of this mess. For all he knew, he would have to keep running for the rest of his life.

He couldn't exactly fight them off. Purdue had probably tried that, and look what happened to him. He hoped he hadn't burned alive, and was already gone when the house burned. That would have been a horrible way to go out.

If Sam didn't want to end up the same way, he just had to heed his last friend's advice. He had to avoid one of the most dangerous groups of people in the entire world for an undetermined amount of time. It would be a monumental task but it was the only way. He just had to keep moving, and hope that Purdue didn't die in vain.

2

THE WITHDRAWAL

Purdue sat outside of the bank on the curb. To most people, he probably looked like some homeless man loitering and looking for some spare change. A lot of people passing by wouldn't pay him a second glance, not wanting to associate with someone supposedly beneath them. They wouldn't even notice the old book in his hands. He did appreciate the people that did stop and offer him some money. It wasn't much, but he honestly would take anything; anything that could get him even a pound closer to getting his billions back.

When the bank opened sharply at eight in the morning, Purdue set about on his mission. It wasn't well planned, and he had few resources, but he knew that plenty of bank robbers got away with far less of a plan. Nowadays, all it took was a note asking for the money and a good disguise. So many had done something so simple and gotten away with it. The only difference was, Purdue wasn't just slipping a note across the teller line. He wasn't just threatening that he had a gun in his pocket and then would demand everything in their drawers. No, he was trying to break into the safe deposit vault.There was a great big difference between robbing a bank and breaking into one. Breaking into one required far more planning and far more skill, and he was lacking in both. Luckily for him, he had something that most people trying to steal from financial institutions didn't have—magic. A little bit of magic might be able to make all the difference in the world.

Purdue had made the sleeping powder. He stuffed all of it into a soggy old sock he found in a dumpster, which made for a surprisingly effective storage unit for the magical tool. As the tellers inside flipped the sign to open, he approached the bank.

He pulled down a makeshift mask he had made from a torn up winter hat he'd found. He ripped holes in it to be able to see through. It sort of resembled a ski mask, but the eyes holes were enormous and uneven, making him look far less intimidating than he hoped. If everything went well, though, there should have been no need to have to intimidate anyone. He could just stroll right on in while his magical powder did the trick.

With his horrible disguise covering his face, Purdue pulled out a lighter he'd pick pocketed from a man a few nights beforehand. Part of him felt a little guilty since the man had clearly been a heavy chain smoker who would miss his lighter dearly. The other part of him though, felt proud to take the lighter from the man, for the man's own health. Maybe his thievery could start the chain smoker's journey toward quitting smoking. It was a terrible habit, after all.

The lighter would be just as good for robbing banks, which was probably a healthier habit to have than smoking toxins. Purdue flicked the lighter on and held the sock full of powder up to the flame. It caught and the fire danced across the fabric. There was a strange smell starting to emanate from the sock and Purdue knew that if he didn't move quickly, he'd accidentally put himself to sleep with it. That would be a terrible start to his redemption. An attempted bank robber passed out at the front door of the bank he intended to victimize. That would be all over the news.

With the smoking sock in his hand, Purdue opened the front door of the bank just enough to fit the sock through and he rolled the powder across the carpet. It took a moment before the powder inside really started to burn and when it did, the sock went up in a puff of smoke.

One of the tellers noticed it and called the others to come help. It was impossible to know what she thought it could be, but Purdue would have loved to hear a guess. He doubted she would have ever landed on the correct answer. A sock filled with sleep powder from a long dead witch wasn't exactly an obvious guess, but who knows, maybe the teller was smart enough to figure it out.

Fumes and smoke filled the bank's lobby almost immediately once the flames touched the powder. As they were surrounded by the fumes, the tellers instantly passed out and fell to the floor. He didn't want them hurt so hopefully they hadn't collapsed too hard. He slowly made his way around the cloud, hopping over the teller stations. He was careful not to accidentally step on the unconscious bank employees. As frustrated as he was with his current financial troubles, it wasn't the tellers' fault.

He moved to a back room that he hadn't been in for a few years; not since he initially put a few private items inside. Nothing too grand, but far better than what he had now. Even his most boring of valuables were better than absolutely nothing at all.

Deposit boxes lined the walls of the room and he looked down the line of them until he saw the number he had been given when he first rented the box: 324. Purdue pulled out his key, which he'd managed to salvage from his destroyed home, and opened up the deposit box.

Its contents were exactly as he had left them: a couple of old scrolls that were rare but hardly worth his time, a large medallion he found in Egypt, and there was the chart that supposedly led to Admiral Ogden's treasure and stolen goods.

Besides his relics that didn't quite make the cut to have been in his private vault, there was a stack of cash. A little over ten thousand pounds. At the time, it had just been spare cash to throw away on a boring rainy day. A minuscule amount in comparison to what he used to have. Now, it was his salvation—the only way he could even start looking for the treasure and the only way he'd ever be able to even get out of Scotland.

Safe deposit boxes were meant to be confidential. As such, the room they were kept in lacked cameras, so the bank and police would have no way of knowing which box was accessed. As far as they would see, a masked man somehow lulled the tellers to sleep and then went into the back and took nothing from the vault. If they tried to do inventory on the safe deposit boxes, it wouldn't matter since they had no record or complete knowledge of what was inside to begin with. He probably could—maybe even should—take some of the money in the vault, but he had his limits. All of this was just about getting back things that were already his. There was no need to actually rob the place.

He shoved the straps of cash into his jacket pockets and rolled up the map before closing the box back up. He left behind the other little trinkets inside. Who knows, maybe they would come in handy at some point someday. For now, better to leave something in the box to make it look like it hadn't been depleted.

Purdue hurried out, practically leaping over the unconscious bank tellers still sprawled about on the carpet. He threw the bank's doors open and looked around, glad to see very few people on the street, and none of them seemed to notice the masked man leaving the bank. That would have gotten plenty of people's attention.

Purdue sprinted down the sidewalk and didn't dare remove the mask yet. Any number of cameras could possibly catch sight of his face if he did. He just kept moving and took a sharp turn down an alleyway.

It was about fifteen minutes later that he heard police sirens. The bank tellers must have woken up from their long nap. It didn't matter, though. They hadn't seen anything. The cameras wouldn't help figuring out whose face was under the mask either.

He'd robbed a bank—sort of—and was getting away with it. He'd actually managed to get some of his belongings back, and that was a first step, an admittedly small one, toward retrieving the rest of his many possessions.

Walton Ogden had come a long way from his days as a simple naval sailor. Back then, he followed orders. Back then, he did as he was told. Back then, he accepted that he had superiors and that he was only going to become mildly successful in life. As a sailor for the Royal Navy, he would never be famous. His name wouldn't be remembered; at best, it would just be one of many on a memorial wall one day for thousands of sailors who served the crown. He had to accept that he would never be rich. His success depended on the actions of those around him. Their choices would dictate his own.

He couldn't stomach that. He wouldn't let his life be restrained like that. Authority was a cage, and the world was far too vast to let yourself be contained in such a small box. He would be as successful as he could be in the time he had, and wouldn't let anything stand in his way. He learned many of his comrades sailing with him felt the same way. They felt just as controlled, and they wanted some freedom. There was one easy way to get it.

They sailed the ocean, an endless void of possibilities. The water could take them anywhere. It could take them to new places that hadn't been touched by the society that was holding them back. It could take them far from old places that they couldn't wait to get away from. They could sail the seas, never staying in one place long. They would be far away from laws and governments.

They could do whatever they wanted. They could be whatever they wanted.

And Walton Ogden wanted to be a very rich man.

He rallied his supporters on their naval ship, rallying them to back him in enacting a mutiny against their stiff captain and all of his many dictations. It wasn't difficult. Most of the crew were on board with doing something for themselves rather than for the country they served. They all wanted a better life, and if they played it right, they would be able to attain the means to improve their lives. They ambushed the captain and those who refused to mutiny, tied them all together with their arms and legs bound, and dropped the whole lot of them overboard into the sea. With their combined weight, the group of them sank rather quickly.

Walton Ogden dealt his first blow to the crown and took control of the ship, with a crew of soldiers who had become turncoats beside him. They had discarded their loyalty to the crown and any oaths they made to the British empire in favor of freedom to do as they pleased. They didn't want to live mediocre lives serving people who didn't even know their names. They wanted something better for themselves ... and this was the right path to take to find that.

They replaced the British flag raised above the ship with a black one, and they pulled down all of the sails, replacing them with red canvas. Ogden wanted something distinctive and dramatic. He didn't want to hide that they were pirates. He wanted it to be very clear what they were and that they had no allegiance to any nation or empire. Crimson sails would stand out against the sky and the blue sea beneath them.

With that, they raided their first vessel, a small little merchant vessel off the coast of Cuba. Taking everything of value on board, Walton Ogden officially became a criminal, and the captain of a pirate crew.

3

AN ODE TO THE LONG LOST PRIVATE
JET

After seeing his bank accounts be drained and erased, Purdue sometimes wished that he had enough foresight to keep more paper money around, tucked under his mattress maybe. But then all of the cautionary tales would have been true and he would have lost it all when his house burned to the ground. There really was no safe place to put his money, expect possibly buried in the ground like a pirate would do. Maybe Admiral Ogden had all of that treasure of his buried deep in the earth and all that mattered was finding a marker shaped like an X.

It felt good to have money again. It was like flexing a muscle that he hadn't used in a while, even if his financial strength was greatly diminished since the last time he bought anything. Unfortunately, most of his money found in the old deposit box was used to charter a flight that would be private and discreet in getting him to Jamaica—the best place to start if the map was any indication.

His passports and identification wouldn't do him much good anymore, so he needed someone who was willing to practically smuggle him into another country. He found that person in pilot Fiona Haddish. She loved flying her plane across the ocean for the thrill of it. Having to sneak into Jamaica was an impossible chance to pass up for someone like her. It would be dangerous, exciting, and memorable. Of course, despite all that, she still demanded most of the money he had due to the risks involved. She may have liked having fun, but like most people, money was still a crucial factor in her decision making process.

Her plane was a small, two-person aircraft. Purdue sat behind Fiona and both wore headsets so they would be able to communicate during the long flight.

The plane rattled during the take-off, but it went smoother once they were finally in the air. They shot through the clouds, leaving Scotland far behind him.

Flying around in a rickety little plane made him miss the private jet he used to travel the world in. He missed the leather couches. He missed the alcohol bar. Most of all, especially now, he missed the walking space. His jet felt more like a traveling hotel room or apartment than it did a plane. It was a far grander than the cramped bucket he was stuck in now.

He took a moment to ponder what happened to his old luxury jet. It might still be sitting on the runway but it was more likely the Order of the Black Sun had blown it to bits. They destroyed everything else he owned after all. Why not take away his favorite way to travel too? If only to further rub salt into the legacy of the man they thought was dead.

"So..." Fiona asked from where she sat in front of him, her voice crackling into his headphones. "What is with this top secret trip to Jamaica of yours?"

"If I told you, it wouldn't be a secret, now would it?" Purdue didn't feel too comfortable sharing his secrets with a complete stranger. With his luck, she was probably a member of the Order of the Black Sun and was going to nosedive the plane straight down or crash it into a mountain peak to kill him. If that were the case, though, then making conversations wasn't going to make a difference. It would at least help to pass the time. "If you really need to know, I'm actually looking for buried treasure, if you could believe it."

"Oh yeah?" The voice in his ear sounded genuinely intrigued. "So, you are going to take a stroll on the beach with one of those metal detectors?"

"Aye," Purdue said. "Something like that."

"Ever find anything good doing that? I've always wondered if it's worth all of the effort that goes into it. Carrying around that equipment and walking all over the place sounds miserable to me."

"I have had a few good finds, yes." He could have told her all about Excalibur, the Holy Grail, or all of the other legendary artifacts that he found over the years, but it would feel wrong, knowing they had all been taken from him. It was too fresh of a wound. "But unfortunately ... I misplaced my box of trinkets and souvenirs."

"That's a shame."

He listened to her inflections closely; and to her tone. It was probably just paranoia but he found himself paying close attention to her responses. Sure, she sounded interested in what he had to say, but only in the polite way when you were trying to make conversation. Maybe if he prodded a little more, to push further to see if he could catch anything stranger than her politeness.

"It was, yes," Purdue said, his ears already perking up in his headphones, waiting to see if what he said next triggered any warning signs. "It was a terrible house fire. I lost just about everything I owned. Felt like it was as all stolen from me."

No sounds came through the headset and Fiona seemed to be sitting real still in front of him. Nervousness crept to the forefront of his thoughts and he tried quickly calculating how he could get out of this situation alive. He could try and take control of the plane and at least land it in the water so there would be a slightly better chance of survival. He could try reasoning with her or even begging her. His mind was racing with worried possibility.

Finally, her reply came through his headphones. "That's horrible. Nothing worse than something like that. My family went through that when I was just a wee babe. Took forever to pick ourselves up. We lost so much."

There were no veiled threats or cryptic replies.

Purdue relaxed a little.

She continued, just as casually as she had the entire time. "So, you're hoping to find something real valuable in the Jamaican dirt to make up for your loss then? If you need money that bad, seems like a waste to have given me as much as you did just to get there. Why not have saved that up and found another way to recoup your losses?"

"Trust me," Purdue said. "The amount of money I need to get my life straight is a hell of a lot more than what I gave you."

"And you think you're going to find that kind of money in Jamaica?"

"I have it on very good authority that I can." The vague etchings of a pirate map wasn't exactly good authority, but like most things, he was taking what he could get.

"Well that's good, at least. Maybe you will give me a ring to pick you up when you make all that money."

Purdue chuckled. "Maybe."

The rest of the flight was easygoing. They talked about all kinds of different things. Fiona went into a long rant about why she had become a pilot and why side jobs like this were the only way for to her make real money. They exchanged stories about their travels all over the world, and the pilot was remarkably well traveled for someone with such a small plane. She took this little engine everywhere. No wonder she was comfortable flying it to Jamaica on a whim.

Finally, she brought the plane down in a long clearing of grass, a far cry from the international runways that Purdue was accustomed to. Once the propellers slowed down enough that they could speak without the headsets on, Purdue climbed out and Fiona called after him.

"Don't you forget what I said," Fiona said. "You find what you're looking for, I hope you'll give me a bit of spare change. I did fly you a hell of a long way."

"I appreciate it," Purdue said. "I'll keep that in mind if I'm feeling generous."

"You be careful here," Fiona called. "People talk about this island like it's changed a lot in recent years. Some new gang, from what I heard. Their leader is—"

"The Wharf Man," Purdue said. "Yeah, I know. He's actually why I'm here."

Fiona looked stunned by that fact, and stared at him with some unease now, like maybe he wasn't the same guy she had just flown over the ocean.

"Is your money worth getting in bed with that guy for? I've heard really, really bad things."

Purdue waved her off and smiled. "Aye, it's well worth it I think."

Fiona frowned. "I hope it's not worth dying for."

Purdue smiled. "I guess we'll just have to find out."

4

THE WHARF MAN

The Wharf Man was something of a legend in the ports of Jamaica. A business man. A crime boss. It all depended on who you asked but one thing that was well known and that everyone could agree on was that no ships left the island without the Wharf's Man permission. He had ships to provide and the sailors who had their own vessels had to pay him a toll or risk their ships inexplicably developing holes that would sink them to the ocean floor.

As such, if Purdue was going to acquire a ship and a crew to get to Admiral Ogden's treasure, he would need the Wharf Man's assistance, and he wasn't overly fond of being in a crime boss' debt. These days, though, Purdue had gotten used to stepping outside of his comfort zone. Desperation and starvation really opened up a whole world of new scenarios.

Purdue traveled to the country's capital, Kingston, where

the Wharf Man was rumored to be based out of. Though he had heard conflicting whispers that he actually traveled all over the island and never stayed in one place long.

He knew that to find a man who was considered to be king of all of the ships in and out of the island, that a dock would be the best place to start his search. He came to the first pier he found, where a handful of men were loading up shipping containers. He approached them and as he did, they all looked at him sheepishly.

Secret crime lord or not, he figured it would be easiest and quickest to just be straightforward. "I'm looking for the Wharf Man. Can any of you lads help me out?"

"The Wharf Man?" The worker burst into a fit of laughter. "You're looking for the Wharf Man? No, no, no, no. No, You aren't. You don't want to find the Wharf Man."

Purdue shrugged. "I really do."

There was more hysterics, like Purdue was the funniest comedian on the face of the earth.

"Hey Nansi!" The worker called to another man lugging a crate across the pier. "Nansi, this man here wants to find the Wharf Man!"

Nansi nearly dropped the supplies thanks to his own fit of laughs. The reaction spread around the docking site until nearly a dozen men surrounded Purdue, all in on some great joke that went completely over his head.

Maybe the Wharf Man was more urban legend than reality. A mistake like that might warrant the mockery he was receiving. He doubted it, though. There were far too many stories about the Wharf Man for him to just be made up.

"Aye, I get it." Purdue held out his arms to the whole pack of dock workers. "You are all truly hilarious bastards. The kings of comedy, really. All of you. But ... all the same, I'm still looking for the Wharf Man."

"Oh, you can stop looking, my friend!" The man was bent over from laughing too hard. The smile he flashed was both amusing but also somehow threatening. "The Wharf Man will find you before you find him. I can promise you that."

There was the sound of something behind him and Purdue suddenly couldn't see. There was nothing but darkness as something was pulled down over his head; a sack of some kind, maybe. He was dragged off of his feet by multiple hands. It felt like he was being dragged through darkness for hours.

Finally, the bag was ripped off of his head and the veil shrouding his view of the world was lifted—part of him wished he could put it back on. He didn't want to have to look at what was in front of him.

An enormous black man sat at a table in front of him. His massive size made the chair he was sitting on look tiny. He must have been over three hundred pounds. The suit he was wearing had to be tailor made for someone as wide as him. Even then, it looked ready to explode off of his body. He reminded Purdue of a rhinoceros in a three-piece suit.

"I take it you're the Wharf Man?"

"I am." When the mountain of a man moved, his little chair rattled beneath him, looking ready to crumble under his overwhelming weight. "I take it you're the man who has been calling for me, hmm? The European man looking for trouble that does not concern him."

"Aye, maybe, but I think the trouble I'm looking for does indeed concern me. In fact, I know it does since it might be the only way I get my life back."

"Your life back?" The Wharf Man's small laugh boomed through the room. "You seem to have life in you right now, no? If you really want your life back, we can help you get rid of it."

Purdue shook his head. "I'm good, thanks."

"So, what happened to your life then? The one you want back bad enough to come bothering me, hmm?"

"Honestly..." Purdue decided to be just that: honest. "A covert secret society of megalomaniacs laid waste to my home and took everything important to me. That included ancient relics I've spent years collecting. That included my billions of pounds of money. Oh yeah, and some of my closest friends. My life, as you can probably imagine, is quite a bit different now. Different enough, that my old life is ... well, gone. That's where it went. I'm breathing still, sure, but this isn't the same life I had before. The one I want back."

The Wharf Man's beady eyes looked at him hard and with some disbelief, but a smile slowly crossed his broad face. "Now that is a story! Secret societies and ancient relics. You are the man with the whip. Indiana Jones. That is you, then, hmm?"

There was some loud cackles from his goons and Purdue felt his hopes slipping away. He wasn't being taken seriously at all. Why should he be? Everything he had seen would be difficult for people to believe under normal circumstances. Now, with how he looked, he didn't have his professionalism to fall back on. He looked just as crazy as he felt on the inside.

"Billions, eh? That is a lot of money, my friend. A lot of money. You must have been a very big man but now you look so small. You telling me you lost billions? How does that happen? Please tell me. You toss it in the trash by mistake, hmm?"

"No," Purdue said firmly. "No, they hacked into my bank accounts. They took every—"

"You had billions. Billions. Now you have nothing. That is a very sad ending to the story. Real sad. So, what then? You come here, looking for me to give you a loan, that right?"

His goons were giggling again, like they were paid to be a good audience for his horrible sense of humor. Come to think of it, they probably were paid to do that.

"Not a loan, no. More like help in finding more money than any of you have ever seen. The treasure hoard of Admiral Walton Ogden."

"Admiral Ogden." The Wharf Man said the name with quiet recognition. "The pirate."

"Aye," Purdue said. He was glad the Wharf Man already knew of him. It might make it easier to convince him to help. "They say the loot he accumulated would be worth millions these days. Given all of the ships his fleet raided, I believe it."

The Wharf Man leaned forward and the chair creaked beneath him. The chair looked like it was using all of its strength to prop him up and support him.

The Wharf Man pointed a fat, stubby index finger at Purdue. "You keep talking about the past. The world's past. Your past. Who you were before you lost everything. Now you are talking about history. You cannot move forward, can you? You are so focused on the past that you can't even see your world here and now clearly, can you, Mr. Yesterday?"

Purdue stood his ground. "The past is important."

"That's only what you tell yourself, Mr. Yesterday."

"Look," Purdue said, ignoring the new name he'd apparently been given. "I need a ship and a crew to help me find Ogden's treasure. They all say the only one who can get those things is the Wharf Man. So here I am, asking for your help. You want me to get down on my knees and beg, fine, I don't really give a shit if that's what it takes."

The Wharf Man let out another booming chortle again. "You want to use one of my ships to go looking for buried treasure. That sounds like a bad investment to me. The chances of you finding this—"

"Are very high," Purdue said confidently. "I have found things that are much harder to find than this. It's what I do. Trusting someone like me with this is far from a bad investment. Given my track record, it's almost a guaranteed success."

"Your track record... what is it you said your name was again?"

Purdue hesitated. It was risky revealing his identity to a criminal like the Wharf Man. He could sell that information to the highest bidder of make it public just to see him squirm. He had the resources to use that name to horrible effect. But, if he was going to win the crime boss over, he would have to be a little more honest.

"My name is David Purdue."

The Wharf Man stared at him, trying to place the name.

"Isn't he that rich Irish man that died some time back."

"Scottish," Purdue corrected. "And yes, that's me."

"You do not look dead to me." The Wharf Man said, but looked ready to hear some kind of explanation, mildly intrigued by the name.

"Like I said, my old life was stolen. I might as well be."

The Wharf Man rubbed his bald head with his fat hand and then plopped it back on the table in front of him with a thud. All of the furniture he was touching looked ready to give way.

The size of the Wharf Man seemed to have its own gravitational force. He could attract followers like the thugs who followed his orders and he could destroy anything that got too close to him.

"And if I give you a ship ... and if I give you some of my men to be its crew, what then, hmm? What is in this for me?"

"A good portion of whatever we find out there. And if the stories are true, then a fraction of Admiral Ogden's treasure would be a fortune. This one job working with me would be more fruitful than any of the little projects you're running out of the docks. That's a promise."

The Wharf Man let out a long breath and twiddled his fat thumbs like he was considering the offer very carefully. "And what would you consider a good portion, hmm?"

"Thirty percent of whatever we find sounds like a reasonable offer, aye?"

The Wharf Man laughed and his whole body rumbled with him. His cronies joined in uncertainly around him, seeming not sure if they should be partaking or not. "Mmm. Very generous. Tell me, what about if you find nothing or very little? My thirty percent would seem very small then, no?"

"If we don't find anything..." Purdue considered that option, and it filled him with sadness to think about. "Then we'll all have lost."

The Wharf Man leaned forward. "Trust is important. I am sure you know this. I need to know that I can trust the people that come asking for favors. I need to know that they are good on their word and that they will not break a deal between us. Can I trust you, Mr. Yesterday?"

"Aye," Purdue said. "You absolutely can. It's not like I have much of a choice these days."

"Good."

The Wharf Man moved with surprising speed for someone of his enormous size, pulling a small harpoon from under the table and slamming it down, wedging it between Purdue's index and middle fingers. It was a precise, calculated move and required an incredible amount of skill to find such a narrow opening and not touch Purdue's fingers. The Wharf Man didn't just have raw strength, he had good aim and alarming reflexes.

Purdue flinched but only slightly. Maybe he was trying to stay calm, or maybe his mind had barely registered what happened because of how quick it was. He hadn't expected a blade to be plunged between his fingers. Now that it was there, he tried to not seem phased. Fear wouldn't do him any good against someone like this.

The Wharf Man looked at him hard, waiting to see a glimmer of terror behind his eyes but Purdue wouldn't let that show. He'd been through much worse than what the Wharf Man was showing. A harpoon was nothing compared to being seconds away from burning alive, or so many other trials he had to face over his many adventures. He would have to try a lot harder if he wanted to truly intimidate him.

The Wharf Man sniffed the air loudly, like he was a bloodhound catching a scent. "Before I give you one of my ships, you need to clean yourself. You smell like shit."

Purdue raised his arm and smelled underneath. Sure enough, he did absolutely reek. Being homeless really did hinder one's personal hygiene.

"Fair enough," Purdue said with an embarrassed smile.

A couple of the Wharf Man's people led Purdue to a shower room and supplied him with a bag of soap, razors, shaving cream, and anything else to help make him presentable and less like a disheveled, dying skunk.

He turned the shower on, and as the water rained down on him, he felt a euphoric amount of bliss. All of the grime, dirt, and stench that had stained his skin since his house burned down was falling off, washed down the drain. He felt so much lighter, and far more like the old David Purdue. Although, he left the beard that was growing on his face. He preferred to have something shroud his face so he wasn't quite as easily recognized.

The shower didn't last as long as he would have liked.

After the weeks he'd had, he could have rinsed off for hours, but the warm water turned cold rather quickly. He forgot how a shower gave you a good environment to think. The water tapped against his head, gently urging to plan, and to remember. The usual thoughts that had been plaguing him were still there. His house in ruin. His collection sealed away in some dark Black Sun vault somewhere. His friends laying in prison cells. But among all of his despair, the water seemed to wash something else into his brain: a little flicker of hope.

He was already on his way to recovery. The first steps had been taken. He had gotten the map back. He got out of Scotland unscathed. Outside of his stench, he was very close to convincing the Wharf Man to give him a ship and a crew.

Purdue almost had everything he needed to really start the search. It just came down to him and his own tenacity. His confidence was shaken after everything that happened, but he kept reminding himself that he had done things like this plenty of times before. The only difference now was his financial circumstances, but he'd already done so much with very little money. He could succeed without his wealth. He knew he could.

Purdue stepped out of the shower, wrapping a towel around himself, only to find that he wasn't alone.

Two men stood in the doorway.

Purdue flinched and nearly slipped on his ass in surprise.

The two men looked identical, obviously twins. They

44

were lanky and tall, towering over him. They had to have been nearly seven feet tall. They both stared down at him with the same eyes. He half-expected them to start speaking in unison, in some creepy way like those little girls in *The Shining*.

Instead, only one spoke. "The Wharf Man would like to finish your conversation."

Purdue wanted to tell the pair off for being a couple of perverts watching him shower. Instead, he settled for something a little less insulting. "Can I get dressed or does the Wharf Man want to talk to me in my damn birthday suit?"

The one who spoke laughed, getting the message, and practically pushed the quieter twin out of the bathroom then closed the door.

Purdue took his time getting his clothes on. He had no problem making those impolite, spying bastards wait for him. When he came out of the room twenty minutes later, the pair of them were standing in the corridor.

Despite being twins, it wasn't hard to tell which was which. One was friendly and spoke while the other was silent and his expression seemed permanently stuck in a glower. He followed the twins down the hall as the outgoing one made conversation.

"I am Alton. This is my brother, Oniel. I do apologize for interrupting but when the Wharf Man asks us to do something, we get it done as quickly as we can."

"Aye," Purdue said irritably. "But you could have at least waited for me to have my pants on."

The one called Alton laughed. "That was our mistake."

His brother, Oniel, on the other hand, didn't apologize or seem to find any humor in the situation. He was looking elsewhere, barely paying any attention at all, probably mad about how long Purdue made them wait for him.

Purdue decided to see what he was really like.

"Oniel, is that right?" The quieter brother offered a glance but no other response. "You're not a big talker, are you?" Oniel's glance narrowed into a glare.

His brother let out another cackle. "He is not, no. Though, I do not blame him. It is difficult to speak without a tongue."

Purdue found himself staring at Oniel's face, maybe hoping he'd open his mouth enough to catch a glimpse of whatever remained inside of it.

"What happened?" Purdue asked but immediately wished he'd hadn't. It was probably a sore subject, and Oniel didn't need more reason to hate him.

"The Wharf Man was in something of a mood one day. My brother here spoke when he should not have. Now he does not speak at all."

Oniel remained still and silent as usual, but behind that veil of passiveness, there was an anger simmering inside.

He couldn't have liked his brother sharing such personal history with a stranger.

The story of the mutilation reminded Purdue that he was dealing with extremely dangerous people. Despite the hospitality he'd received, including allowing Purdue a long overdue shower, the Wharf Man was not a merciful individual. No matter how well he was treated by his enemies, he had to remember that.

Purdue mused quietly. "Alton. Oniel. Such interesting names in this place. So what's the Wharf Man's name, eh? Or is Wharf his first name and Man his last? Is it Mann with two 'n's? Is that it?"

Neither of the twins smiled at his weak joke, not even a little. The Wharf Man was clearly not someone who liked to talk so glibly about. He wasn't someone to speak about when joking around. When it came to their boss, they knew to tread more carefully than that.

They brought him back to the Wharf Man who greeted him like they were the best of friends. After that business with the harpoon almost spearing his hand, maybe they were now. "You had a good wash, hmm?"

"Aye," Purdue said uncomfortably, tempted to mention the twin voyeurs outside the bathroom. "The water pressure was wonderful."

"I am glad to hear it and I am also glad that we understand each other, yes? If you think about turning on me ... after I was nice enough to give you one of my ships and a shower ... I will poke out your eyes and then tie your feet to rocks. Drop you in the water, where you won't be able to see, but you will be able to drown. I promise you."

"I know how it works," Purdue said. "You don't have to worry about me stabbing you in the back. It's not really something I do. I'm the one who tends to pull the knife out of my back. So, maybe it's you I should be worried about."

The Wharf Man's chubby face scrunched up and then he released a booming bellow that shook the whole room. "I like you, Mr. Yesterday. I will get you a boat and a crew to man it."

Within twenty-four hours, the Wharf Man had prepared a crew and was having a boat supplied for their voyage. While everything was being made ready, the Wharf Man insisted that he get to see the map that Purdue had gotten from the safe deposit box.

Purdue didn't really want to show him, but decided it best to be as open with his new business partner as possible. They sat down together, and he opened up the old map, then rolled it out on the table.

"I have given you one of my boats, but I realize now that I don't even know where my property is going. If we are going to proceed, I need to know where its destination is."

They looked over the chart together. The Wharf Man

leaned forward and looked ready to fall over from the shift in weight.

The map was a crude sketch of land masses around the Atlantic Ocean. There were Xs sketched all over the map, and the Wharf Man let out a growl of annoyance. "I do not understand this. The X is supposed to be the treasure, no? So, this pirate admiral of yours hid all of his gold all around the Atlantic? Divided it in dozens of places?"

"That's what you think at first glance, isn't it?" Purdue said, having believed the same thing when he first saw it. "But I don't think that's the case. Because of this..."

Scrawled on the bottom corner of the map was a sentence in cursive: *It is protected by my sword and gun powder*.

The Wharf Man still looked more than a little confused. "What good is a map if it does not show you were to go?"

"I think it does ... but it's just not obvious. There's something here. Something with that note. It's always slightly intrigued me. It's why I could never get rid of it."

"So, you know what it means?"

"Not exactly," Purdue said honestly. "But I have a hunch, and that will be the first stop on our voyage."

INTERLUDE 2 – SAM CHECKS OUT

Just like every morning, Sam woke up in a bed that wasn't his. It was more comfortable than some of the others he had the displeasure of sleeping in lately. Still, no matter the conditions he was now forced to live in, it was better than being killed. It was far better than what David Purdue got. No matter what motel he was in, his morning routine was the same. Sam would wake up, get himself dressed, and sit by the window with a cup of coffee. He'd always make sure his car could be seen from whatever room he was staying in, and would check to see if any cars were parked near his. He didn't want to be jumped on his way out.

It was a challenge to be running from pursuers that you weren't even sure were after you. All he had to go on was Purdue's warning, but it wasn't proof that the Black Sun was coming for him. For all he knew, they didn't bother with him and he was running away for no reason, keeping one step ahead of an invisible enemy that wasn't even there.

But he knew Julian Corvus, and if he was leading the order now, then he doubted that man would let any slight against him go unanswered. He hadn't let Purdue get away. He probably hadn't let Nina either. So, why would he leave Sam be? He was just as much of a part in his defeat back in Norwich as Purdue and Nina were. And Sam had been just as much of an enemy to the Black Sun.

No. They were coming. They had to be.

There was a knock on his door. "Housekeeping."

When Sam opened the door, a woman was waiting on the other side. Her name tag read 'Marie', and she greeted him with a pleasant smile. Her cart of supplies was behind her, and she looked past him at the state of the room. The truth was, he'd barely touched the place besides the bed. The room was spotless otherwise.

"I should be all set today, thank you," Sam said, glancing around the parking lot for any occupied cars that might be spying on him. Marie obviously noticed his eyes and looked around herself, like she was expecting something frightening, but saw nothing. "Come back tomorrow."

"Of course, sir," Marie said. "Have a nice day."

"You too."

Marie smiled at him again and rolled her cart of cleaning supplies away. Sam peered around the area one last time before retreating back into his room. Usually, he liked to only stay in one place for one night before moving on to somewhere else. But lately he'd expanded that window to two nights sometimes. Caution was good, but that extra day helped him recuperate from the energy he was using by being constantly on the move. He would spend one more day there, and then pack up and get moving again.

It had occurred to him that the way he was hiding could only last so long. Motels cost money and unlike his late friend, Purdue, he wasn't a billionaire. Eventually, his wallet wouldn't be able to keep helping him stay hidden. When he came to that point, he wasn't sure what he was going to do. Hide out in some forest somewhere like a modern day Robin Hood? Find some cave somewhere to hole away in? It was hard to say what would come next. Thankfully, he had enough to keep up this plan of his for some time.

Part of him wished he could just call up Julian Corvus and ask if he was even coming for him. He could save himself all of this trouble if he at least knew that he was actually being hunted by the Black Sun. Another part of him wanted to call up his old neighbors and ask about the state of his home; if it had been broken into, ransacked, or burned to the ground like Purdue's had been, but he also didn't want to risk contacting anyone. He wouldn't put it past the Black Sun to somehow be able to track him down through a phone call. It was part of the reason he had destroyed his cell phone the second Purdue had told him that he should start running.

Sam spent the day keeping to himself, mostly in his room, and only leaving to go get food or gasoline for his car. The solitary life was difficult at first. He had felt completely cut off from society. Other people he passed on the street had their own lives filled with happiness, sadness, good times and bad, but he doubted any of them were in his situation. They probably didn't have some secret society out trying to track them down and kill them.

He'd had plenty of ups and down in his past, but this was one of the most challenging points in his life. He had to constantly be on the alert and that was draining, but it was all for his own good. It was the only way to avoid what happened to Purdue.

So, when he returned to his motel room, he gave one last cautionary look out the window before tucking himself in to try and find some sleep. Rest hadn't come easy in a long time, but he forced himself to push out the thoughts that a Black Sun agent could be standing at the foot of his bed, or would murder him while he slept. Like the rest of the world, he couldn't run all the time, and those hours of sleep made him vulnerable to the enemies there were potentially looking for him at all hours of the day.

But sleep was just as essential to his survival as looking out the window or over his shoulder, so he forced his body to recharge for the next day of trying to survive.

The next morning, there was a knock on Sam's door. He slowly rose from his bed and got to his feet, tiptoeing to the window and barely peeking out, just enough to try and see. Luckily, it was just housekeeping. The same woman he'd seen going about the other rooms earlier in the day.

"Hello?" came a voice as another knock came. "House-keeping, sir."

"One moment," Sam said and pulled open the door.

Marie stood in the doorway just like she had around that time the previous day. She tried to smile at him but for some reason, her face wasn't quite cooperating. Actually, she looked scared for some reason. As he looked at her, he could see she was even trembling where she stood.

"I am sorry," she said.

Two men appeared around both sides of the door frame. Sam tried to slam the door shut on them but they got in its way, keeping it open. He pushed desperately in a vain attempt to keep them out, but he knew it would be futile. Their ambush was too quick and too strong.

So, the Order of the Black Sun finally tracked him down. He should have known it would be sooner rather than later.

He'd been so careful too ... damn it all. He should have stuck to always moving every single day. It was that extra night that had cost him the chase. He had stayed in one place too long, giving them time to catch up.

At least now he knew that the order really was after him. He didn't have to wonder if all of his running was for nothing. He didn't have to even consider going back home. Purdue's warnings had been right and it was Sam's own fault for slowing down.

In the brief glances he could get of them, the two intruders didn't look familiar. It figured that Purdue got to have Julian Corvus himself come pay him a visit, and the Order of the Black Sun only sent the expendable grunts to deal with Sam. He would have been insulted but he was too busy trying to keep them out.

He couldn't hold off two grown men throwing themselves against the door for long, but he braced his whole body against it. The men outside threw their bodies at the door, trying to bash it open. Their attempts rocked Sam, but he kept himself firmly pinned against the entrance, keeping it at bay as best as he could. Hopefully, the two men didn't burst through the motel room windows. There would be no stopping that.

He shouted at them through the door. "Whatever you are selling, I'm not interested!"

His hold of the door slipped and they burst through, breaching his motel room, and knocking him backward. He reached for whatever he could, his hand instinctively going for the bedside lamp. He flung it forward but they easily avoided it.

"I think you have got the wrong room," Sam said as the two men closed in on him. They both looked like wild animals ready to pounce on their prey. They were lions and he was just some helpless antelope in comparison. He just tried to stay calm and collected. Panicking wouldn't help him at all. "I don't remember ever ordering any room service."

"You're coming with us," one of them said. "Now."

Sam took a step back. "No, no I really don't think I am. That doesn't sound like something I'd ever do, to be honest."

"This isn't up for debate." The other man reached into his jacket and pulled out a pistol. "Let's go."

Sam put his hands up in surrender. "Right then. How did you find me?"

"We've been on your trail for some time. You were just

lucky to be one step ahead of us and that luck has run out. Mr. Corvus is looking forward to seeing you again."

"I bet he is." Sam lowered his hands. "But is the Order of the Black Sun really going through all this trouble for me? I doubt I would be of much use to you all now. You apparently killed my colleague with all the real resources."

"Mr. Corvus thinks otherwise."

They grabbed Sam and practically dragged him out toward their car.

He passed the maid who had brought them to his room, and Marie mouthed the word 'sorry'. She didn't look overly apologetic though. A little guilty, maybe, but the Black Sun had either paid her well or put her in a position where there was no other alternative but to give him up.

"One-star service," he muttered to her as he walked by, although felt bad about it immediately after. This wasn't her fight, and the Order of the Black Sun was quite persuasive when they wanted to be. Just like he was trying to maintain his own survival, so was she. She wasn't going to risk that for some man she barely knew, customer or not.

They shoved Sam into the back seat of a car and he knew all of his running had reached its end. He was finally caught and at the mercy of an enemy he knew all too well. The Order of the Black Sun was going to settle old debts just like they had with Purdue, and Sam wished more than anything that he was in his own car, driving to a new motel somewhere far out of reach.

Unfortunately, no seedy motel could help protect him now.

Sam had no idea where he was being taken and he didn't bother asking. He had enough experience with the Order of the Black Sun to know that they weren't the most reasonable of people. He sat in the backseat of the car quietly, knowing that this vehicle was really just a prison cell.

The larger of the two Black Sun operatives, Ulrich, drove the car while the other, Roland, sat beside Sam in the backseat. His hand rested under his coat, probably on his gun holster. The body language spoke so very loudly to Sam. It warned him not to dare try anything.

"You're a tough man to track down, Roland said from beside him. "You didn't make it easy, I tell you. Staying mobile was a good move. I must say, I was impressed."

"I wasn't," Ulrich said from the front seat, glaring at Sam through the rearview mirror. "More annoying than anything. We were supposed to have brought you back to Mr. Corvus weeks ago."

"You been kidnapping people for Julian a lot? My friend Nina was missing, last I knew. You abduct her too?"

"The doctor lady?" Ulrich asked with a chuckle. "No."

57

Sam felt some relief but then Ulrich continued. "Mr. Corvus saw to her personally."

Sam's hopes plummeted. That was the worst possible scenario for Nina. Julian Corvus was a demented lunatic in regular circumstances. Nina had almost killed him—maybe had even completed the task before his miraculous revival—and he had more than enough reason to be even worse than usual to Nina. Julian wasn't the forgiving kind, and who knew what depths he would go to avenge his own death? He would probably torture Nina. He would kill her slowly. Maybe he already had.

Sam trembled at the possibilities that were happening to Nina.

"Yeah," Ulrich snickered. "She's our prisoner too."

"Guest," Roland corrected facetiously. "Our valued guest who accepted Mr. Corvus' personal invitation."

"Right," Ulrich laughed. "She is our honored guest and we have had her since before we beat that bastard, Purdue."

"I thought Purdue died in a house fire," Sam said, knowing full well what the truth was. He would play dumb because he wanted to hear these monsters say it. He wanted to know how they had done it, so that someday, he might be in a position where he could do the same to them.

"Oh, it was indeed a house fire," Ulrich said. "Quite the fire."

"You saw it?" Sam asked. "You were there?"

"I was there, alright," Ulrich said with a disturbing amount of nostalgia, like he was reminiscing about some great deed from the past. "That was a fun evening. You should have seen it. Drove trucks right through that castle of his. Knocked those walls down real well. That David Purdue, the little rat that he was, went scurrying away to that trophy room of his. That door was so thick, it could have probably taken a nuclear blast and still have been standing. It was a damn panic room, really."

Sam clung to each word. As much as he hated the story and how he knew it was going to end, he needed to know the full truth. For his own peace of mind, he needed to know how Purdue had fallen. He'd escaped death so many times, why was this time different?

When Purdue had called him warning him that the Black Sun was back and that Julian Corvus was alive as their new leader, he had probably been holed up in that room Ulrich was talking about. If it was as impenetrable as they described, how the hell did they get in? Or why had Purdue left the safety of that room?

Almost on cue, that was starting to be answered for him.

"We tried to use your friend, Dr. Gould, to lure Purdue out but even then, he refused. Selfish bastard cared more about those dusty old trinkets of his than protecting his friend. He would have left you hanging too, I'm sure."

That sounded like Purdue, but given how powerful some of those "trinkets" were, Sam couldn't blame Purdue for refusing to hand them over, even when Nina's life was on the line. Nina surely understood that just like Sam did. The contents of Purdue's collection were far too valuable to willingly hand over.

"Lucky for us, we had a woman on the inside, and she was in that trophy room with Purdue. I don't know how, but she overpowered him and opened the doors right up for us."

Anger simmered within Sam. Even with all of his improvements to his security, Purdue was still too trusting. Whoever that woman they were talking about was, she had cost Purdue everything: his relics, his home, and his life.

"She let us in and we ransacked that trophy room. Robbed that rich man of all the riches he was worth, didn't we?"

Roland smiled. "We sure did. And that rich man was worth quite a lot."

The two Black Sun agents were so proud of their great, big, evil secret society defeating just one man. They had no right to be smug about it. They should have been embarrassed that it took them so long to get rid of him. Even now, they had trouble just tracking Sam down. Those motels had protected him far longer than he expected them to.

"I couldn't believe some of the fun toys he kept in that room. Spears taller than me." Ulrich spoke like it was some old fable, not caring about the details. Things dug up from the country of 'who cares', that were originally from the year 'who the hell knows when'. Put most of what we have in our vaults to shame."

"Purdue put your order to shame in more ways than that," Sam said under his breath.

That shut the two of them up for a few seconds but they quickly recovered. "He didn't look so great when we had him tied down to a chair in his own house. We made him watch when we packed all of his things up. Took everything of value he had. Walked right by him with a crate full of his old shit. His face ... I'll never forget that face. He looked like a little boy getting his blanket taken away. Then we doused his walls with gasoline. Then lit the whole place up real good. Last I saw him, he was about to cook real nice."

Ulrich sniffed loudly. "Mmm. Can practically still smell him now. Can you?"

Sam's blood was boiling. It was bad enough that they were acting so arrogant. It was even worse that they were practically spitting on Purdue's grave. On the one hand, staying their captive meant possibly being brought to where Nina was. On the other hand, he didn't want to give them another win.

David Purdue was the thorn in the Order of the Black Sun's collective side for so long, and now he was gone. And here was Sam, probably going to be killed by the Black Sun too. If so, he was going to die just as Purdue had, remaining just as sharp of a pain in the secret society's ass.

"You're all terrible people, you know that?"

Before Ulrich or Roland had a chance to respond, Sam threw himself at Roland in the back seat beside him. He grabbed hold of the side of his head and slammed it against the car window. Roland groaned when his head smacked the glass and, in the confusion, Sam pried the pistol out of Roland's holster.

Ulrich roared and slammed his foot on the brake, bringing the car to a screeching halt. Sam lurched forward from the abrupt stop, almost fumbling the firearm. He barely managed to keep hold of the pistol, and pointed it at Ulrich before he had a chance to draw his own weapon.

"Don't," Sam ordered.

"You're not going to shoot," Ulrich balked, still reaching into his jacket.

"No?" Sam fired a shot right past Ulrich's ear. Both Black Sun agents held their hands over their ears, as the sound of the shout bounced around the inside of the car. "Try me."

"Okay! Okay, goddamn it! You probably burst my ear drum!"

"Good," Sam said. "Gun. Out the window. Now."

Ulrich was still groaning from the pain in his ears and

frantically rolled down his window, dropped his pistol out of the car, and then put his hands up. Roland was holding his own head, where he was bleeding from where his head hit the glass window.

Sam held the pistol firmly in his grip, not shaking at all. He finally had control of the situation, and he was going to make sure that his newfound influence on everything going on wouldn't go to waste. Who knew if he'd ever get another chance like this? He pointed the gun at the driver's seat, at Ulrich. "Drive."

"Where?"

"I don't know yet," Sam said honestly. "But I've got the gun so it doesn't really matter does it?"

Ulrich groaned but then stepped on the gas. The car moved forward and for the first time since being on the run, Sam Cleave felt at ease.

5

OUTSET OF A VOYAGE

The boat wasn't large but it would work for the task ahead of them. The crew seemed just as capable, with a dozen people hired by the Wharf Man to find Admiral Ogden's treasure.

As he watched his new crew mates arrive and walk up to the gangplank to the ship, he was reminded of the colleagues he used to travel with: Dr. Nina Gould and Sam Cleave. They both had a passion for history, or at least for discovering truth. They didn't need to be paid to take part in Purdue's exploits. Just helping to make discoveries was enough for Nina and Sam. His new colleagues only cared about their paychecks.

He hoped the two of them were alright, but he doubted it. Nina was a prisoner of the Order of the Black Sun, and that secret society had claimed that Sam would soon join her. By now, he probably had, and the two could be rotting in a cell being tortured, or they could be in even worse shape. His friends needed him more than ever and he needed that treasure to help save them, but it would be so much easier to even find that treasure if Sam and Nina were with him.

A tall woman with a shaved head came up the gangplank and shook Purdue's hand. "I'm Aya, and will be your first mate on this voyage."

"Pleasure to meet you," Purdue said. "I hope you know how to navigate a ship better than I do."

"Of course," she said with a wink. "I have been sailing since I was a child."

"Brilliant," Purdue said, feeling more at ease.

"So I am told we are looking for some kind of buried treasure? Is that right?"

"Well, we don't know for certain that it's buried," Purdue said coyly. "But yes we're looking for a treasure hoard that an incredibly successful pirate amassed centuries ago."

"And you know where this treasure is?"

"I have the map," he said, not exactly answering the question. "I will speaking with the whole crew shortly to make sure that we're all on the same page."

A familiar voice called from the dock, "Mr. Yesterday!"

Purdue looked over the side of the boat to find the Wharf Man standing on the pier. It was a wonder that he could even walk around at all.

"Do not forget my words. Do not cross me, my friend."

"I won't," Purdue said. "You will see your thirty percent in no time."

"I better," the Wharf Man snorted. "But you can never be sure, they say, hmm? So I have made sure to give you the best of the best."

The twins who brought Purdue to speak with the Wharf Man appeared and strolled up the gangplank, past Purdue. Alton grinned a wide, bright smile as he walked by but Oniel looked just as irritated as ever.

"They will be of great help to you," the Wharf Man said. "I am certain."

"Thanks," Purdue said quietly, really not feeling thankful at all.

"We are just going to make sure things go as planned," Alton snickered, patting Purdue hard on the back. "We are to be the Wharf Man's eyes, ears, and I'm going to be his voice as well, since my brother cannot." Oniel didn't look amused by the jab, but he never seemed amused by much.

The Wharf Man waved them off, again reminding Purdue to not betray him as the ship took off. It was good to know that there was trust between them at the start of the voyage.

As the boat pulled away from the docks and headed out to open sea, he gathered the crew on the deck. None of them looked very excited to be there. To them, they were taking part in an imbecilic treasure hunt that was going to lead to nothing. It was all just a waste of time in their eyes.

The Wharf Man probably thought something similar, but couldn't resist the slim chance that it wasn't a wild goose chase. He was probably sitting at home expecting Purdue to fail but hoping that he would come back with a ship full of valuables.

Purdue cleared his throat. "I have in my possession ... a map." Purdue held up the rolled up old parchment. "And this map leads to what is supposed to be the largest hoard of stolen treasure that any pirate had ever accumulated. More than Edward Teach, better known as Blackbeard. You might have heard of him, aye? More than Calico Jack. More than Captain Kidd. This treasure was collected by Admiral Walton Ogden. Some of you may have heard me tell your boss about it, but those who didn't, Admiral Ogden commanded the largest pirate armada that ever existed. An entire fleet that could spread across the sea and pillage and plunder all over world simultaneously. And in the times when the ship did come together, their fleet was strong enough to take on even the strongest naval forces of the world."

Some of the crew looked impressed. Others seemed bored like they were just listening to some old fable.

"Admiral Ogden's fleet managed to get their hands on an absurd amount of gold, pooled from the plunder their ships collected. Nowadays, that loot is worth millions. And I tell you right now, no matter what the Wharf Man is paying you ... you will also all receive a portion of that from me. A substantial portion. Each."

Their expressions brightened and there was a palpable excitement coming over everyone on board. Purdue knew this was the way to win their loyalty. If he could offer something even better than the Wharf Man, they would follow him and help him get to their prize. It was too enticing for them to resist. It was the best way to start a voyage with a ship full of untrustworthy criminals.

"We will find the treasure together, and will all reap the rewards. I promise you that."

There were cheers and applause after that. Purdue felt a surge of relief. He'd known far too many stories about mutinies on ships. He hoped this would satiate this crew of complete strangers enough that they wouldn't even think about committing one against him. He preferred to have this voyage go smoothly, without his lifeless body being tossed into the sea.

Purdue stepped into the captain's quarters and was surprised to find someone else already occupying it. Aya sat on the little bed against the wall, flipping through an old black book. Purdue recognized the tome almost immediately. It was Mona Greer's book of shadows.

Aya stared down at the book with wide eyes as she turned each page. Purdue understood that expression, and was sure he looked just as horrified when he saw the book's contents. The rituals described inside were enough to fill anyone with terror, maybe even enough to drive someone insane. He was always very careful with it and kept himself from looking too long.

Aya didn't understand that. She didn't know how dangerous the book was and had no inclination to be cautious with it. She was transfixed, her mind being pulled in by that witch's vile imaginations. She didn't dare look away. As fascinated as she was, though, the rest of her body was trembling.

Purdue took a step closer and she looked up at him, but her gazed seemed like it was straining to stay on him; like it was being pulled back toward the pages against her will.

"Wha—what is this?"

Purdue took another cautious step in her direction. "Something you really shouldn't be reading. What are you doing in here?"

Aya ignored his question, still transfixed on the book in her lap. "Are ... are you some kind of devil worshiper?"

"Not at all." Purdue walked to the bed and plucked the book of shadows out of her hands. He snapped it shut. "Believe me, this thing scares me just as much as it clearly scares you. It was written by a witch centuries back and, as I'm sure you already saw, is filled with all kinds of nasty dark magic that you want nothing to do with."

"Why do you have it then?" She asked, her lips still quivering. "If it frightens you?"

Purdue looked down at the bindings of the old spell book. "Because there have been times when I needed it. And there may be times ahead when I need it again. Also, it's kind of the last remaining piece of my stolen collection. As horrible as it is, it does have some strange sentimental value for me, I admit."

Aya eyed the book and shook her head, still staring at it as Purdue tucked it out of sight in his bag. She looked worried that the journal was going to pull itself back out.

"I do not like it," she muttered.

"Neither do I." Purdue made sure the book was out of reach before returning to his question. "So what were you doing in my private quarters?"

"I was looking to speak privately about this next part of our search."

"The flintlock?"

"Yes."

"What about it?"

Aya rubbed her shaved head uncomfortably. "We were instructed to man this ship. To be your crew as you used the boat to look for the pirate's gold. No one said anything about stealing from a museum, putting me and my men at risk."

"I wasn't expecting to have to steal anything either." He was being completely honest, but stealing was becoming a somewhat worrying trend throughout this quest for

Admiral Ogden's loot. First he robbed a bank, now it was going to be a museum. He was practically begging to be imprisoned. "But it's the only way to get to that treasure. You were tasked with helping me find it, right? And this is part of that."

Aya glared at him. "None of us want to take the risk."

"Oh please," Purdue said, rolling his eyes. It was harsher than he usually was but he didn't need insubordination right now. "You work for a crime boss. You don't think I know what the Wharf Man is all about? Extortion. Smuggling. Probably things much worse than that. He's your boss. Risk of arrest is part of your job."

Aya glowered at him but he could tell that he struck a chord. He finally made a point that she couldn't brush off or deny.

"If this goes badly, Purdue, this crew does not forgive easily."

"But it does forgive, aye? That's good," Purdue said, but Aya didn't looked at all amused. "Believe me, this is going to work out just fine for us. Besides, the Bahamas are supposed to beautiful this time of year. Let's try to enjoy it."

The red sails of the *Scarlet Wing* were infamous long before the vessel was the flagship of a pirate fleet. Its crew were notorious cutthroats and thieves who attacked ships and ports so frequently, many wondered if it was out of some sadistic compulsion that need to be satiated.

Walton Ogden's ability to command such a crew earned him respect from other pirates and fear from just about everyone else. They had gained enough of a reputation that others flocked to them, to join or offer deals of allegiance. All of those others wanted a piece of what the *Scarlet Wing* was able to obtain. No other ship was as effective at pillaging and plundering. On that ship, with its sails as red as blood, victory was always a guarantee.

As the crew's numbers grew and they captured vessels to accommodate that growth, they altered the crew to help manage the newfound fleet. Jacob Morrow became captain of the first ship they added to their ranks, the *Iron Horn*. Having been Ogden's first mate, Morrow was entrusted to make sure that Ogden's commands would be carried out, even when he wasn't on board himself.

As their fleet grew and each ship was captained by very capable pirates, the important decisions all still came from the *Scarlet Wing* and from Walton Ogden—who had been proclaimed as an admiral by the nearly dozen ship captains that followed him.

The overwhelming raids that the fleet committed overshadowed the exploits of other like-minded pirates in the Bahamas; even the most feared ones like Blackbeard and Edward Low. Those pirates were respected and feared in their own right, but unlike Ogden, they didn't have firepower that could contend with entire nations.

The whole world was talking about Admiral Ogden's armada of vicious murderers. News of their various ventures spread, being told on every continent, in almost every country known to man. Their assaults on ships carrying wealthy passengers, robbed blind by a group of ships led by one with red sails. Their battle with a small fleet of British war ships that should have been able to defeat them, but somehow were all sunk by the pirates.

And their most legendary of feats: the ransacking of a coastal British fort that supposedly housed a large cache of gold, a naval treasury. They took control of the fort, and used the cannons on its battlements to sink anyone that tried to approach. They didn't leave until they stripped the entire fortress of anything of value. When they were done, the entire fleet bombarded the fort with cannon fire until its structure gave out and it collapsed.

The fleet of pirates quickly became something of legend and their leader was even rumored to be a myth. After all, could any one man really lead that many criminals and killers?

One of the moments in Admiral Ogden's life that history would never talk about happened on the night of a hurricane, where all manner of people gathered and huddled together inside of a rickety old tavern by the sea. Ogden wasn't on one of his many adventures, or raiding expeditions, which he would be known of for centuries. He wasn't standing at the helm of his infamous vessel, navigating the storm by himself. It was a rainy and mundane night that helped define who he was.

It was the meeting of strangers, who for years would only cross paths for a few minutes; for one conversation that would have profound effect on the pirate for the rest of his life.

Ogden sat away from his crew like he often did, watching the various groups of people who were trying to weather the hurricane rocking the island. A drink in his hand, he wasn't really in the mood for any sort of conversation. He just wanted to try to be patient, and wait for the hurricane to subside so he could head back to open sea, and scratch that itch that kept bugging him—the need to go out and take as much money as he could find. Even now, he had half a mind to order his crew to start robbing everyone in the tavern, but even he wasn't cruel enough to do that while everyone was trying to stay safe in the storm.

There was a young woman walking toward him, looking out of place compared to the rest of the room. She just didn't look like most of the females inside the tavern. She carried herself in a peculiar way compared to the others; a rehearsed and proper way that none of them could even begin to try and attain. The daughter of some wealthy family that would never have been in a place like that unless it was the only choice they had. No, she wasn't one of the women begging for attention from the sailors passing through. She wasn't someone waiting for payment for her various services. She wasn't doting with her beauty to increase her station in life. No, she looked inquisitive and had a pleasant, welcoming smile. It was too nice of a smile, showing that she clearly was from somewhere else, where smiles were still genuine. She was an altogether different kind of woman than the ones Ogden had grown accustomed to in recent times.

She took a seat across from him at his lone table and he had stared at her peculiarly. She was focused on watching all of the other antics going on; like the cheers and fun his crew was taking part in. She looked confused by it all, and seemingly too distracted to realize that she had just sat down with someone else.

"Anything I can do for you?" Ogden asked, with a cough.

She looked a little startle by his greeting but then her expression shifted to a polite nod of acknowledgment. "No thank you. I am just curious."

"Curious about what?" Ogden asked, finding himself genuinely intrigued by her. It had been a long time since a woman had practically ignored him. So many wanted the validation of a famed pirate who was becoming known all over the world.

"My father heard a rumor." She nodded toward a well-dressed man standing in the corner of the other side of the room, looking more than a little uneasy about the company he was being forced to keep. "He heard that these people here are pirates."

Ogden laughed. "Well, it is quite a common thing to be in these waters, as I'm sure you know."

"Of course," she said. "Quite common sadly. I hear such horrible things, but they have always captured my curiosity. And according to my father, these men are not the usual rabble of scoundrels you see hanging around sometimes."

"No?" Ogden asked, feigning innocence, and taking a sip of his rum.

"No," she said, looking at all of them with wonder and amazement. "My father said that these pirates serve under Admiral Walton Ogden himself."

Ogden almost spit out his drink but just managed to keep himself together. If this girl only knew who she was speaking to. Ogden looked at his crew like they were all strangers and he was just as fascinated by them as she was. "Is that so?"

"If my father is right, then yes." She almost trembled with excitement, even giddiness. "I wonder which one he is. You have heard of him, yes?"

"Of course," Ogden said with some pride. "Who hasn't?"

"Then you have heard what they say about Admiral Ogden? I've heard so many things."

"I'm afraid I don't," Ogden said awkwardly. "I admit, I can be oblivious to a lot of everyday gossip. Please enlighten me. How does the civilized world see him?"

She straightened her posture like she was about to recount some amazing tale. "They say that Admiral Walton Ogden commands a million cutthroats on thousands of ships."

That was a bit of an exaggeration that made Ogden smile. People always seemed to have a way of making impressive things sound somehow far more thrilling than they already were. He had just about a dozen vessels under his command, a far cry from thousands, and he couldn't even begin to imagine trying to be in charge of a million people.

"They say that his personal ship, the *Scarlet Wing*, has red sails." That much was true. At least, all of those buffoons got something about him right. Then she continued, "They were dyed red with the blood of all of his enemies. That he drained them dry of their insides and painted his canvas with it." There was the ludicrous fable that he expected. Was it really so hard to believe that his sails were simply made from red fabric? They had to make him sound like such a sadist.

"I have also heard that he was never born, at least by usual standards." That was a strange one, and he found himself excited to hear the rest. "That he was spit out from the bottom of the sea, that he is not a man at all, but instead a monster from the depths that wants to kill any and all who breath air above."

"A monster, eh? So he is what ... some kind of fish man?" Ogden asked with a snicker, impressed with whoever came up with that one. "I wonder if he has scales."

"I am not sure," she said, far more serious than he was being. She really believed some of these stories. This was why more of the so-called "civilized" people needed to see more of the world. Instead, they stayed in the comfort of their homes and believed all things outside of their domain were outlandish and unheard of, when in actuality, the truth was far less of a spectacle. "I have heard one story that said that Admiral Ogden could sniff out gold on a ship, like a bloodhound, and that was how he collected so much treasure. He was drawn to the gold."

It wasn't exactly true, but the basis was accurate. He did have a keen ability to collect vast amounts of treasure.

She kept looking around at all of the crew, probably trying to deduce which man was the admiral himself. Most of her possible choices were embarrassing themselves with drunken antics, looking like fools more than famed pirates. That was where the struggle seemed to be. No man in the tavern radiated with some otherworldly glow of greatness that would indicate their identity as Admiral Ogden, not even the true pirate himself.

This young lady obviously didn't believe that such a sadistic, scaly-skinned pirate monster from the bottom of the sea would be enjoying a quiet drink by himself.

"What is he supposed to look like?" Ogden asked, enjoying this game far too much to stop now. He would see it through for however it long it took for her to recognize the truth. "Surely, someone said something about him."

"Not particularly," she said, sounding disheartened. "Some pirates ... all they talk about is what they look like. Edward Teach and the matches that he sticks in his great black beard. Jack Rackham and the calico clothing he wears. But Admiral Ogden ... no one has really said."

That was a shame, Ogden thought. Maybe he just needed a more defining physical aspect. As she said, some men like Blackbeard derived their reputations heavily from how they looked. He didn't really have that distinguishing feature that made him stand out. His claim to fame, his fleet of pirate ships, wasn't exactly something he could wear.

"Well, what do you imagine Admiral Ogden looks like?"

"He would have to be quite intimidating to command a whole fleet of pirates," she said, almost whispered, musing over the question. "A mountain of a man, I would think. Tall and strong."

Again, Ogden almost burst into a fit of laughter. He wasn't particularly tall and he wasn't particularly strong. Most wouldn't call him intimidating either. In fact, he tried his best not to be most of the time. If he tried to intimidate his crew, he would only meet with resistance. No, he discovered long ago that being understanding and charismatic was the only way to gain the respect of his men. He could be fierce in a fight, but he never stomped around like he was the strongest man on the seas. In fact, plenty of his own crew were stronger than him. He just had their trust, and their loyalty. That was where his strength came from.

"I can promise you, Admiral Ogden is not nearly as tall as you're imagining."

She turned to him for the first time and they met eyes. It was like she had barely recognized there was an actual person sitting across from her before. Just the vague shape of some vagabond sitting in a tavern; someone beneath her status in life, who she would speak to, but didn't have to actually look at.

"And how might you know that?" she asked, still looking fascinated. "You have met him?"

"I have, yes," Ogden said. "In fact, I am part of his crew."

"You're with them?" She asked, turning back to the celebrating pirates. It was probably baffling, to think that someone as quiet and isolated as him would be working with a rabble like that. "You serve in his fleet?"

"I do," Ogden said honestly. If she wasn't going to figure it out for herself, then he was just going to have to steer her in the right direction. "I actually serve on the *Scarlet Wing* itself. She's docked out there, you know? Trying to make it through this horrible storm. I'm sure she will be just fine. She's seen much worse."

"You've served on it for long?"

"Since the beginning, yes," Ogden said.

"Tell me all about it, I must know," she said, leaning forward with wonder in her eyes. "Are the sails really stained with blood?"

"No," Ogden said. "Whoever told you that has a wicked mind, though."

"But what of the admiral? What is Admiral Ogden like?"

Ogden had hardly ever been asked to describe himself, and he never even cared to think about himself that much. So much of his thoughts and energy were directed outward toward various things. He had to always be thinking about the crews under his command. He had to be thinking about how they were going to contend with the sea on a daily basis. He had to think of strategies for the fights that always were ahead. He had to even be thinking about how best to keep his treasure hidden. He barely gave himself any real thought.

Even so, he did his best to at least give it a try. "First of all, he is not nearly as monstrous as you have been led to believe. He does not collect the ears of his enemies or tie naval soldiers to anchors and drop them into the sea. All of that is nonsense. No, Walton Ogden is a man just doing his best to find some success in life. Just like anyone else. It is his only real desire. To be rich and famous." The young woman listened carefully to every word, and surprise crossed her face upon hearing that all of those rumors were so incorrect. "He is the type of man who doesn't mind sitting by himself at a table, and speaking with a young lady who should really not believe everything she hears."

Her eyes widened and the rest of the tavern disappeared now. He wasn't invisible to her anymore. He was the only thing that she wanted to look at. He wondered if she was disappointed by what she saw since he didn't quite live up to all of the fables that she had taken so much value in.

The view of Admiral Ogden from the populace was far different than the man himself. She almost looked like didn't believe him at first, but the longer her gaze lingered on him, the more seemed intrigued.

"You?"

Ogden let himself laugh aloud this time and shrugged. "Me. Yes."

"I'm ... my apologies," she said, bowing her head courteously. "You're just not at all how I pictured you in my mind. I'm afraid I just didn't know."

"Evidently not," Ogden snickered. "That is quite alright. Now that you know my name, it's only fair that I know yours."

"Of course! Yes, I am Victoria Hart." She was red from embarrassment, now averting her eyes to try not and stare at him.

"It's a pleasure to meet you, Victoria," Ogden said holding out his hand in greeting. She slowly took it and he brought her hand to his lips where he lay a gentle kiss on her knuckles. He then looked passed her at her well-dressed father across the room. "What brings your family to this island? Besides this damn typhoon?"

"My father runs a trading company. He brought me along just to see how he conducted his business properly. We found shelter here when we saw the storm brewing in the horizon."

"It's a good thing you did," Ogden said. "I doubt most

vessels can survive out there against something like this. Not even us."

"How many of you are here?" she asked. "Surely, I would have seen thousands of ships."

"That's yet another fact about me that you were mistaken about," Ogden said. "I don't have nearly that many in my fleet. Not even close. But no, right now it's just my ship docked at this island. The others are raiding all over the world. We won't see them for quite some time."

"Your ship really is here? The *Scarlet Wing*? How did I miss it!?"

"Its sails are up right now," Ogden explained. "And given that moments ago you thought that those sails were dripping with blood, I can see why you wouldn't take any notice of it."

It was a bit of an insult but Victoria didn't seem offended by it. In fact, she seemed annoyed with herself for acting like such a fool in front of someone who she was so intrigued by. She still seemed overwhelmed that she was sitting at the same table as a man she had thought was some sort of monster manifested from the sea itself. He was hardly the type of company she usually kept.

"Can I ask you something?" She spoke hesitantly, like she was afraid to say the wrong thing.

"Sure," he said. "It's not like I'm doing anything else right now."

Victoria still looked uneasy about speaking to him

directly. It seemed to be a lot easier for her to talk about him when she thought he was someone else. Now, with the most direct source for answers, she seemed extremely hesitant. Maybe she thought a cutthroat like him would murder her if she said anything offensive.

Finally, she spat out her question. "Why do you do it?"

"What do you mean?"

"Why are you a pirate?"

That particular question was something he never gave much thought too. In the few times that he had thought about what set him on that path, he always thought about wanting to be free of anyone giving him orders when he had been in the navy. He wanted to be free to do whatever he wanted. He wanted to find his own course for success.

"I wanted to live my life without anyone telling me I couldn't do it that way," Ogden said. "I wanted to be able to make myself whatever kind of person I wanted to be without proper society judging me. I wanted to be as free as the ocean allowed me to be. So that's exactly what I did."

"But do you have to be a ... a criminal ... to do that? Breaking our laws. Do you do the things everyone says you do? The stealing, and the fighting ... the killing?"

"Some of them, yes," Ogden said. "But the worst things I only do when I have to, usually when there's no other choice. Freedom always has a price. And sometimes that price can be take a heavy toll on you."

"I imagine you are able to pay any price, are you not? With the amount of money they say you have stolen..."

"Yes," Ogden conceded. "I suppose that amount of gold does help."

"Why take it? Why hurt so many people just to get gold? Why not find work instead? That's how the vast majority of society does things. Your line of work can only end poorly for you in the end."

"We'll just have to see."

"So when this storm passes..."

"We'll do what we always do. We will pillage and plunder for whatever we want from whomever we want. For instance, when you and your father are on a ship heading to wherever it is you're heading ... that's exactly the kind of ship we would target. A whole ship full of well-off civilians who wouldn't be able to stop us from robbing them." She looked away again and Ogden chuckled. "What? It's the way the world is, I'm afraid."

"I suppose," she said. "It was nice to meet you."

She rose from the table and Ogden put his hand on her arm. She flinched and looked down with fear but relaxed when she realized he was holding her wrist rather gently.

"It was nice to meet you too, Victoria," Ogden said. "I'm not nearly the monster they've made me out to be am I?"

"No," she said uncertainly. "Not nearly. But perhaps still a monster of some kind. A beast that feeds off blood and gold until he gorges himself. Perhaps that kind of a monster. Safe travels, Admiral."

"You as well."

With that, Victoria walked away, leaving Admiral Ogden alone at the table once again. He watched her return to the well-dressed man across the room who was staring over at Ogden curiously. Ogden wondered if Victoria would tell her father who he was. He kind of hoped so, just to see the rich man's face when he realized he was looking at the supposed sea monster in human flesh that doused his ship's sails in human blood. Given that he didn't look nearly as curious as his daughter, he would probably be terrified, far more afraid of the pirate than she had been.

Although, that image she left him with did stick in his mind very thoroughly. The image of a beast drinking blood and gold until it had its fill—there were some days when that really did resemble him. But other days, quiet ones like this, with someone to have a good conversation with...

6

THE PLACE PIRATES CALLED HOME

The capital of the Bahamas, the city of Nassau, was renowned for its role in the history of piracy. It had been a hub for all kinds of seafaring criminals during piracy's golden age. Many notorious vessels made port there and used it as a home base when raiding the waters around it.

Now, Nassau was a booming tourist attraction and vacation destination. Cruises stopped there to let their passengers off for a day of tropical fun and sightseeing. People could enjoy its beaches and waters, including its beautiful coral reefs that many liked to dive to. They could enjoy amazing food at all kinds of exotic restaurants. It was the perfect place to relax and it was a far cry from the rough, dangerous island it used to be.

There were no longer pirates running it. There were no longer war ships with black flags on their masts docked in the harbors. There were no longer battles between the British royal navy and the notorious pirates that had practically taken control of New Providence Island. All of those historical battles were now just fodder for the museums to use for their exhibits. The age of piracy in Nassau had long since passed.

But it hadn't forgotten its history. Its association with the pirates of old still permeated its streets and shores. There were countless tourist spots dedicated to teaching the history of piracy and an obnoxious amount of gift shops selling foam swords and rubber eye patches. Purdue wondered how many of those worthless souvenirs and toys kids really needed.

It had always bewildered him how pirates had been romanticized over the years. Bloodthirsty murderers and criminals had become heroes of adventure. It was strange how much perception changed over the centuries.

The Nassau pirate museum was far more expansive than the pirate museum he recently visited in Salem. That made sense. Salem was a town that used to have frequent run ins with pirates, while Nassau had been something of a pirate metropolis.

There were all kinds of exhibits and displays with items that had been collected long ago. Pirate relics had probably been easy enough to find in a place like Nassau. They were probably strewn all about the island for any passerby to be able to pick up. They had probably had enough antiques to open up a museum with the moment they decided to create one.

Purdue and the crew spent their time at the museum taking note of the security. They counted cameras. They looked over the entrances and windows. They observed the security guards who were lightly dispersed throughout the museum.

Purdue knew that they needed to account for every possible scenario that could happen, and they needed to know everything they could for that to matter. To everyone else, they were a group of tourists enjoying the history on display around them. In reality, they were seafaring pirates themselves, preparing to make off with a valuable possession and then make their escape at sea.

Purdue stumbled upon a glass display all about Admiral Ogden and some of the collected items related to him were inside. Apparently, all of the items inside were collected from the shipwreck of Ogden's sunken vessel, the *Scarlet Wing*, and had been hauled up and donated to the Pirate Museum of Nassau years ago.

They even had the pirate admiral's sword. The blade had been warped and debilitated from its time in the water. It was crusted over with coral and rock. It wouldn't be able to cut a carrot now, let alone pierce the body of a human being. It wasn't the proud weapon of a pirate anymore. That's what centuries did to a blade in the ocean, though. It turned it into nothing more than a relic from a time long past.

The flintlock that was on display didn't look much better. In fact, it hardly looked like a gun at all anymore. It could have easily be mistaken for a piece of driftwood. Its centuries being battered by the currents and pressure of the sea had forged it into a new shape. The wood of the old pistol had been made smooth and withered. Its edges had been scraped up so that the barrel of the weapon now ended at a series of sharp points of wood.

The etchings that Admiral Ogden had carved into his pistol were very faded but still present. Under closer inspection, they could probably be read, but not from behind a glass case.

"Can't you read it from here?" Aya asked beside him.

"Absolutely not," Purdue said. "We'll need to get a much better look."

Aya looked more disappointed than surprised. She probably hoped that they could get whatever information they needed as tourists, rather than thieves. It was a far less dangerous route, but unfortunately for them, thievery was their best option.

They spent the next day preparing for the heist. Despite their involvement in the Wharf Man's seedy enterprise, no one on the crew had much experience in such high level thievery. Everything they planned seemed like it would work in theory, but no one knew for sure how things would go once it was being carried out; once it was really happening. No one had ever been part of a job like this before so no one could offer than any useful advice.

They were going to be going in blind.

If something with the plan went wrong—and there was a high chance that something would—then their whole operation would implode. Any chance of getting any closer to Admiral Ogden's treasure would be gone too. They needed this flintlock to help decipher all of those Xs on the map. Everything relied on getting that crusty, rotting piece of wood that barely resembled a gun at all anymore.

While they prepared, Purdue filed through the book of shadows looking for anything that could help make their heist easier. The sleeping powder he used at the bank wouldn't do him much good this time, and even if it could, there was no way of collecting the ingredients he needed from their ship. No, he would need something else, but the witch's journal mostly just offered tortured methods or ways to murder people. Not even magic could help this makeshift, amateur heist go well.

There was a time when he could have just thrown his money around to make things easier. He could have paid off a security guard or bought a private tour of the pirate museum. He might have even been able to just purchase the old flintlock from the museum itself with a big enough offer.

Not anymore. He was practically crippled now. He and his crew had to rely on thievery alone, and none of them were professionals.

The Pirates of Nassau Museum closed promptly at nine o'clock. Purdue and the crew were going to wait at least an hour after that to start their operation, just to ensure that any straggling tourists or workers were away from the museum. The less people they had to worry about, the less obstacles they had to manage to avoid, and the easier the whole thing would go. Given their collective lack of experience in stealing from museums, they needed everything to go as smoothly as possible if they were going to succeed. One hiccup in the plan and the whole job could collapse in on itself, taking all of them with it.

At ten o'clock, under the cover of the night sky and the quieting streets, the crew took their respective positions that they had all been assigned. Purdue waited across the street at a bus stop, looking on his phone and pretending to be waiting for his transportation.

The others were spread about as well. Aya and Alton were walking on the sidewalk, holding hands. Aya hadn't been overly thrilled with having to pretend to be romantically involved with Alton, but he took the assignment in stride and was playing it very convincingly. He laughed and danced around with her in the street like they were enjoying a lovely date night in the city of Nassau.

Oniel, on the other hand, used his typical silence to his advantage and sneaked up to the museum. Despite knowing the path he was going to take, Purdue still barely noticed the mute man as he crept up to the building and started climbing up to one of the windows.

There were only going to be minimal security guards inside, two or three at most, so it wouldn't be too difficult for a man like Oniel to deal with once he was in the building. Purdue did stress to him though that killing wasn't a necessity.

"It would make things a lot easier," Alton had argued.

Purdue didn't care. He knew he was working with dangerous people who had probably used lethal force to their advantage plenty of times. But those guards were just doing their jobs, protecting items they probably didn't even know much about. They didn't deserve to die just for wanting a paycheck.

Hopefully Oniel respected that. He hadn't been able to argue verbally like his twin brother had, but his expression at the time had made his opinion on it very clear. He wasn't happy about being told how to do his own job, especially from someone like Purdue who had no real authority over him.

Oniel's task was to break inside, either sneak past or take down the guards, disable the security cameras, and open the door from within. Trying to break in through the front door would have set off a number of alarms and ended their operation before it even began. Oniel needed to help open the floodgates so they could get in without a full blown siege on their hands.

Oniel scaled the side of the museum and used some saw-like device to cut a hole in one of the windows. Once there was a big enough opening for him to fit through, he disappeared into the building, out of sight. The success of this operation was all on him right now. The rest had to be careful later on, but the beginning of it was one of the most crucial parts. If he failed, they all failed, like a series of dominoes falling on one another.

Purdue remained firmly seat on the bench across the street. Every fifteen or so seconds, he'd glance over at the museum, hoping he'd see Oniel's signal. Aya and Alton continued their giggling and little dances on the sidewalk, pretending like they were having the time of their lives but each time Alton spun Aya around in a little romantic twirl, she was really checking for the signal just like Purdue was.

Every minute that passed while they waited, Purdue felt more and more nervous. If Oniel had been caught, then it was all over. They would never get in and one of the most skilled people on the crew would be lost to them. And who knew what Alton would do if his brother was compromised. Based on what Purdue had seen, he would probably move heaven and earth to get his twin back, even at the expense of the mission.

Finally, one of the lights in the museum flashed on, and then off, a handful of times—the signal they were waiting for. Oniel had succeeded in getting inside. The door was unlocked. Purdue breathed a long sigh of relief from where he sat on the bench. All of those worries he had felt in those last minutes faded away, and now his anxiousness was fixated on the future. The first part of the plan had worked. Now they just had to make sure the rest of it did.

Purdue casually strolled up to the museum. Aya and Alton were a few steps behind him, trying not to make it look too obvious that they were altogether. Purdue reached the door and it was pulled open in front of him. He entered and Oniel was holding the door for him.

"Well done," Purdue said, glancing around for any sign of dead bodies. "Are the guards still breathing?"

Oniel, as usual, said nothing but just glared at Purdue. It wasn't exactly and answer so when Purdue walked into the museum's lobby, he made sure to keep his eyes peeled for wherever the guards ended up.

Alton and Aya came in soon after, and Oniel locked the door behind them. Purdue turned around to greet them and the four of them all stood there in the empty museum. He took a moment to appreciate the fact that things were going well so far.

"So far, so good, hmm?" Alton snickered.

"Oniel, you keep watch," Purdue said.

Oniel nodded but as usual looked annoyed that Purdue was ordering him around. Alton patted his brother on the back. "Just do as your told, brother. This will be easy."

Purdue, Aya, and Alton hurried through the museum. They moved toward the exhibit that Purdue had examined during their visit earlier. It was tucked into one of the museum's corners and in that exhibit, the display of Admiral Ogden's recovered belongings waited for them.

The coral encrusted cutlass. The worn down flintlock that had been nearly turned into a useless piece of drift-wood. Old navigational tools, silverware, and chests that had been found in the sunken wreckage of his ship. It was all there, all ripe for the taking. Among all of the valuable items from the age of piracy in that museum, Admiral Ogden's was worth the most. His possessions weren't valuable themselves, but if they led to his treasure, as Purdue suspected they did, then they were worth far more than anything else. They were worth as much as the riches that they could help find.

"Aya, can you check on the guards please?" Purdue asked, as he looked over the display. "Make sure they're still breathing."

"My brother did not kill them," Alton said firmly.

"And how do you know that?"

"If Oniel killed them, believe me, you would know," Alton chuckled. "You would be able to tell right away and wouldn't miss it. There would be much more of a mess. A great, big mess."

That wasn't exactly comforting. "Please," Purdue said again to Aya who nodded and left to go find the guards.

This next part of the plan would be more challenging than infiltrating the museum. They had to actually acquire the items on display without triggering any sort of alarms or giving away that there was anything unusual going on in the exhibit.

Alton had managed to pick up a device through the Wharf Man's connections on the black market. A tool used by some of the world's most skilled thieves that could open up glass cases, without triggering the alarms that were set to go off if they were broken into. They hadn't exactly been able to test the tool's effectiveness, so there was a great risk performing the trial run during the moment when they actually needed it.

It looked almost like a giant wrench, with adjustments that could be made to its u-shaped jaw, to adapt to whatever it needed to grip. Alton pulled out the wrench and fit it to the size of the security glass that stood between them and Admiral Ogden's items. The claws of the wrench gripped the glass tightly and then Alton pressed the button on his device.

Once the wrench was attached properly and firmly to the case, Alton put in ear plugs and handed Purdue a pair of them so he could do the same

The tool's biggest asset was that it could release a high frequency sonic vibration, which could easily shatter glass into tiny pieces in seconds. It was incredibly useful to completely destroy a glass barrier so quickly, that the alarms wouldn't even register that the glass was damaged or gone. A perfect tool for someone who needed to get something inside of a glass case.

Alton pressed the button and the glass display instantly

shattered. The glass fragments left behind were so tiny that they seemed like nothing more than sparkles as they fell away from the items they were guarding.

Purdue waited a moment and then removed his ear plugs, somewhat expecting to hear alarms blaring when he did. There was nothing. The tool seemed to work exactly as intended. Alton turned and smiled at Purdue who couldn't help but return it.

Their plans were really working.

Suddenly, alarms started sounding all throughout the museum.

"Shit."

That wrench was supposed to be fool-proof, so either the tool didn't work, or they were fools. Either way, they were in deep water.

"Hurry," Purdue said, grabbing the old rusty cutlass and putting it into the case that they had brought along to carry the items. He made sure it was secure and then grabbed the driftwood flintlock as well. The message Admiral Ogden left hinted at the need for the sword and the gun, so as long as they had both of those, they should have be good. Alton, however, was taking everything else in the broken display case and tossing it in their case. "What are you doing?"

"Being certain," Alton said over the alarms. "Would hate to have missed something. Better to have it all, hmm?"

Purdue didn't disagree but they didn't have much time

until the police arrived. They had to get moving. Aya came running into the exhibit. "What happened!?"

"Bad advertising," Alton said, removing the wrench from where it was clamped and shoving it into his jacket. "I will have that man's head for selling it to me."

"That's if we make it out of this," Purdue said anxiously, locking his case with the sword and gun inside. "Let's get the hell out of here. Right now!"

The three of them sprinted through the museum, back toward the entrance. As they ran, Purdue noticed a few of the security guards on the floor in the corner of his eye.

"Aya, are they alive!?"

He didn't want the law enforcement on their way to have even more reason to hunt them. Dead security guards would only make things harder for them.

"They are," Aya replied. "Oniel just knocked them out."

Oniel was standing in front of the museum's entrance where red and blue lights could be seen flashing outside. They didn't need to worry much about the security guards. They had bigger concerns since the police had already arrived.

"There has to be another way out of here out back," Purdue said.

Alton took a step toward the front door, next to his brother, and then stopped. "Will not matter if they have already set up a perimeter around the whole building."

"Then let's get out of here before they do!" Aya said, quickly falling into a panic as the walls seemed to be closing in around them.

They hurried toward the back. There had to be a better exit, maybe a maintenance exit for the workers for when they loaded new attractions into the museum. They managed to find one at the very back of the museum, down a long narrow corridor past the staff break rooms. Oniel kicked the door open to the outside, when there was a shout behind them.

"Stop right there!"

A security guard was behind them, with police officers flanking him. They were about a fifty yards down the corridor. Purdue held the case with the artifacts inside tightly and then pushed his allies forward out the door. They needed to put more distance than that between them and the authorities.

"Split up, get back to the ship as quick as you can," Purdue said as they all hurried out into the city. Purdue sprinted into an alleyway, while Oniel, Alton, and Aya all chose their own directions and dispersed. Unfortunately, the streets weren't crowded enough this time of night to simply disappear into the crowd. They had to really hurry.

The police and security guards couldn't be that far behind. He glanced back as he ran to see if any were following him, and sure enough, there was a couple of policemen running in his direction. He could hear sirens dispersing in the distance, trying to chase down his friends in their cruisers. Hopefully, his three crew mates could handle themselves.

They had what they needed now. He just had to keep going and get to the ship. The heist hadn't gone exactly as planned, and this was a sticky situation he was in now, but once they were out to open waters, they could put this mess behind them. It would all just be a slight bump in the road on their quest to find Admiral Ogden's treasure hoard.

Purdue kept running with the long carrying case in hand. Hopefully that brittle old sword wouldn't break apart from this whole ruckus. It probably hadn't been moved in years. It was more than fragile, and now it was caught in the middle of a chase.

The guards were close behind, practically on his heels. The operation wasn't going as well as he hoped, but was close to what he realistically expected. When did any plan work perfectly? Nothing was easy when it came to finding rare artifacts. It never had been. There were always going to be bumps in the road; or in their case now, rough waters ahead.

Purdue scurried down another street, and he kept looking back every few seconds to see if his pursuers were still there. He could see them, pushing their way through passersby. He made for the docks as quickly as he could. When he got there, he sprinted across the pier and nearly leaped up the ship's gangplank in haste. His crew were all gathered, helping him get aboard. He could see Aya, Oniel, and Alton among them.

"Is everyone here?" Purdue gasped out, looking around the deck and then back down at the approaching guards. "Are we all here?"

"Yes," Aya said, looking past him at the police officers and security force running down the pier.

Purdue yelled out, "Well come on then! Raise the anchor or whatever the hell we need to do to get the hell out of here now!"

The crew hurried and pried the mooring lines off of the dock. The engines came to life and hummed beneath them as they ship slowly pulled away from it had been docked. They were breaking away from the shore, out to sea just in time.

A couple daring policemen leaped from the dock in a fleeting attempt to catch them, but the ship was inches out of reach. They missed the boat and tumbled down into the water with a splash. Some of the crew cheered triumphantly as they left their pursuers back on dry land. Even Purdue joined in. If he didn't feel like a criminal before, he sure did now.

"That could have gone better," Aya mused beside him, staring at the police swimming back to the pier.

"Aye," Purdue said, but then shrugged. "Then again, it could have gone much, much worse."

He put the case containing the cutlass with the other

ones they had taken from the museum. They now had all of Admiral Ogden's belongings, and hopefully a way to decipher his maps. It may not have gone smoothly, but their hodgepodge of a plan did succeed, and that was all that mattered right now.

A voice rang out behind him. "Don't move!"

The whole crew instinctively disobeyed the command and turned around to see who was giving it. A policeman was pointing a gun at them. Water dripped off of his face and his clothes were soaked. He'd obviously managed to cling onto the ship even after his dive from the pier. Purdue was slightly impressed.

The officer repeated his order, this time more firmly. "Do not move."

Purdue took a step forward, hoping he could talk his way out of this one. His crew mates watched him with concern; they actually looked worried about him. That was surprising and even made him feel a little good despite the gun in his face.

Purdue put his hands up. "There's no need for the gun, friend. You caught us. Fair and square."

"Do not move!" The policeman repeated again, his face glistening with sweat or salt water. "Don't."

"Alright, alright," Purdue said.

The policeman was young and his mannerisms spoke to his inexperience. The gun was shaking in his hand and his eyes were filled with trepidation. He wanted to do his job, but he didn't want to shoot anybody. All of this must have been his first real action since he joined.

"You have the controls, aye?" Purdue offered helpfully.

"Don't move!" The officer barked. "Please! Just—"

The policeman let out a horrible gasp, like the air had just been forcibly exorcised from his body. His gaze was wide with surprise and fear as he crumbled to his knees.

Oniel rose from behind him, having quietly made his way to the policeman's blind spot with the same silence he always acted with. Purdue hadn't even noticed him sneak back there.

The officer dropped his gun and his eyes rolled to the back of his head, as he collapsed onto a heap on the deck. A large red stain was spreading along the back of his shirt.

Oniel stood as tall as ever with a bloody knife in his grasp. He peered down at the fresh corpse without any visible reaction. The entire murder was done with such calm collective attitude that it sent a shiver down Purdue's spine.

"The hell did you do?!" Purdue snapped, still reeling from the past thirty seconds. An innocent, law-enforcing person killed for trying to stop criminals; for doing his job and trying to stop criminals. Now he was dead, and who knew what he left behind?

"What he had to do," Alton answered for his twin brother, walking out from the group of spectators. He crouched down and picked up the dead officer's pistol. He removed the gun's ammunition clip and chucked it into the sea. He then tossed the gun itself overboard. "My brother protected this ship and protected the Wharf Man's investment. Oh yeah, and he protected you. I think you should be thanking him."

Purdue didn't want to. He didn't want to be in that creep's debt. He could have gotten them out of it and he could have done it peacefully, with just a conversation. Instead, those twins had to ignite unnecessary bloodshed. They killed an innocent man and were acting like it was a good thing.

Alton and Oniel each picked up two of the policeman's limbs, raising him up as blood still fell from his body. They carried him over to the ship's railings, ready to throw him overboard just like they had his gun.

Purdue moved forward to stop them but was too stunned to take any further action, as they heaved the body over the side and dumped it into the ocean.

When the twins looked back, they could obviously see Purdue's disapproval written all over his face. Alton snickered under his breath and gave a casual shrug. "What? The sea is a fine place for a private burial."

"They'll never find him..." Purdue said, realizing that the police officer would be considered a missing person for some time, and eventually considered dead, but there would be no evidence. No body for his family to bury or burn. There would be nothing physical to mourn, just a feeling that he was gone, and a slim hope that maybe he could return some day.

"So?" Alton asked with a confused smile, like Purdue was playing him. "Go ahead and say some final words for him, if you really want. He can't hear you, though, so what is the point, hmm?"

There were giggles from some of the crew. Purdue could feel the respect he'd earned from them slipping away just a bit. He was being treated like a pest by the twins, but this was his venture, not theirs.

Alton looked past Purdue to address the rest of the crew more directly. "The Wharf Man told us to make sure no one got in the way of him getting his money." He waved his hand toward the water, where the police officer's body was probably sinking to the ocean floor. "That man there got in the way. We will do the same thing if anyone else does. Anyone."

It was a warning to the crew; a threat even. That much was clear, and Purdue's shipmates looked rightfully mortified by Alton's words.

In that moment, it occurred to Purdue that while the crew was full of criminals who were willing to steal and smuggle, and break laws, they weren't stone-cold murderers like the twins clearly were. Neither of them batted an eye when they so callously disposed of the policeman. No wonder they were the Wharf Man's most trusted lieutenants. They were willing to cut someone down without hesitation. The boss must have loved that.

They were efficient tools to use when he wanted something. Precise, and most importantly, sharp.

The casual way they committed horrible violence—killing even—reminded Purdue of Julian Corvus. The twins shared his tactic of using sudden acts of aggression to make a point. They were the same brand of monster. The only difference was they lacked Julian's ambition. That was good. They may have been beasts but they at least still had someone they answered to.

Alton and Oniel walked through the crowd of shaken crew members. They brushed past Purdue and he could almost feel how cold they were, as it was radiating off of them.

Oniel would probably have stuck his tongue out at him if he still had one.

Despite Purdue having the map and leading the expedition, it was obvious who was really in control. It was the Wharf Man's ship, after all, and through those twins, his big grubby hands were still all over it.

After successful raids, the pirates who were part of Admiral Ogden's fleet would meet with their flagship to collect what they managed to plunder during their own ventures. The rules were simple and Admiral Ogden made sure that they were followed. Everything valuable would be handed over to him, no exceptions, and if it was discovered that any of his fleet were withholding or hiding any of their loot, the punishment could be incredibly severe. The rules were strict but fair, and most of the ships in Ogden's fleet respected and followed those rules without any resistance. They all knew who was in charge, despite their vast numbers.

As far as where the gold went after it was pooled together, that knowledge was left only to a chosen few, hand selected by Ogden himself. And many of them vanished entirely after transporting the gold to wherever Ogden took it. Not even the other captains were privy to the exact location of what must have been the biggest hoard of treasure ever collected. Maybe it was paranoia but Ogden preferred to think that it was just being sensible. He couldn't have anyone decide to go take all of his hard earned money while he was sailing the high seas.

Everyone seemed happy enough with the fair share he gave them of the loot. It was always a good cut of it that allowed them to enjoy their lives, when they weren't risking their lives on the high seas.

The only exception, it seemed, was his former first mate, Jacob Morrow, who seemed more and more frustrated by not having any direct access to the gold that he help acquire. He was a cunning seaman, and the ship he captained, the *Iron Horn*, was one of their toughest vessels. Ogden should have expected that his old friend would confront him about being left in the dark at some point.

As three crews from their fleet gathered at a tavern in Nassau after a lucrative raid, Morrow took a seat at the corner table where Admiral Ogden had been sitting alone. Their crew mates in the tavern around them all drank, laughed, and sang together all around them. Their lone table in the corner was noticeably quiet and dour in comparison to the rest of the place.

Morrow poured himself a drink. He didn't offer any to Ogden. The two men sat in silence for a number of minutes, with Morrow downing his drink while Ogden stared at him from across the table.

Finally, Morrow spoke what was so evidently on his mind. "What exactly are we going to do with all of this gold?"

"I'm not quite sure what you mean," Ogden said passively, not wanting to get too defensive.

"I mean that we have more money than God himself and we just keep taking more, and more. What are we doing all of this for at this point, hmm? You saving up to buy yourself your own private country? Your own continent? The whole world itself?"

"No," Ogden said honestly. "What are you on about? There's nothing wrong with making a profit."

"Maybe not, but you do have to wonder why we put so much effort into making it when we have enough gold to live like kings for the rest of our days. All I'm saying is ... there comes a time when it starts to feel like we're amassing all of this wealth for no reason other than to be able to say that we have."

Admiral Ogden raised a brow. "You think we're wasting our time."

"I think we're wasting our energy," Morrow corrected. "Sure, having mountains of treasure is great but it's worthless if we don't use it. Especially if we don't use it to get to somewhere better than where we are now. To purchase something big or to increase our station in life. We've gotten so much, yet ... how better off are we now than we were when we first started?"

"Have you lost faith in me, is that it?"

"No," Morrow said with some exasperation. "I haven't lost faith. I just want to know why we are sitting idly by on a gold mine and not doing a damn thing with it. It's started to feel like you're just grooming your ego."

"My ego?" Ogden laughed but Morrow wasn't laughing with him. "Then you and anyone else who doubts me are just going to have to trust me and my ego a little longer."

Morrow didn't look very pleased with how the conversation went, especially since he didn't even get a straight answer about what was going to be done with the gold.

Ogden wasn't bothered by Morrow's feelings. He didn't owe anyone any explanations, no matter what position they had in their fleet. They just needed to learn to be more patient and to trust in his capabilities. They needed to remember that they might have been captains of their respective vessels, but he still had complete control over those ships.

They all worked for the gold, yes, but Admiral Ogden was still the leader of all of them. As such, it was his responsibility to make sure that their prizes were safe. He would see to it that they all received their fair share eventually. For now, insubordination wasn't going to help keep that treasure safe. He only trusted himself to make sure that its location wasn't compromised.

His treasure had to be kept safe.

INTERLUDE 3 – SAM IS TURNED UPSIDE DOWN

"I'm going to be running out of gas soon."

Sam didn't respond to Ulrich's complaining from behind the wheel. He'd been listening to him and Roland moan and groan ever since he essentially took them hostage. Taking people hostage wasn't something he had much experience in, but he made an exception when those hostages were otherwise murderers and sociopaths who had taken him hostage first.

Sam didn't have a plan. He wished he did, but nothing was coming to mind about how to proceed. He had the gun in his hand, and he had two Black Sun agents held hostage, driving him to an undecided destination. They'd been driving for hours. Part of Sam didn't mind that. He had already avoided capture by staying mobile and bouncing from motel to motel. Staying entirely mobile in a car helped ensure his safety even more ... but it couldn't last long. He needed a plan and he needed one very, very soon.

"Pull over up ahead."

"We're in the middle of nowhere," Ulrich growled.

Sam waved the pistol in his hand at the rear-view mirror. "Just keep going."

At least he was the one holding the gun, dictating the situation, but outside of using it on the two operatives, he didn't know how else to really get out of this predicament. If he ditched them and stranded them on the side of the road, he was sure they would eventually track him down again. They did it once before. If they were as good of hunters as they claimed, then it would only be a matter of time until he was their prisoner once more. Only next time, they would make sure he didn't get the gun. This was his only chance, and he couldn't waste it.

Roland didn't look very nervous. In fact, he looked more at ease than he had the entire time Sam had the gun. It seemed like things had somehow improved for him, even though he was still Sam's hostage. "There's something you should know about us, Mr. Cleave. I think you will find it quite interesting."

"Yeah? And what's that?"

"You of course already know that the Order of the Black Sun has people everywhere. I mean everywhere. It's quite the network of members dispersed all over the globe."

"This isn't news to me," Sam said. "Purdue and I fought your friends in all kinds of different countries. It's a real pain in the ass that all of you Black Sun goons seem to just sprout out of the ground. I already know you all have a disturbing amount of members in your club."

"Of course, of course," Roland said with an amused cough. "But, as you can imagine, communication can be difficult with that many members. We need advanced tools to overcome that challenge. Ways to be able to get the order's attention when we need. A way to know each other's' locations in case of an emergency. A quick and easy way to send messages."

A wicked smile stretched across his face, like he was the only one who knew the funniest joke in the world. In the rear-view mirror, Ulrich's smile was visible as well, and it looked just as triumphant.

"For instance..." Roland continued.

He pushed his sleeve up. A high tech watch-like device was wrapped tightly around his wrist—and it was blinking red.

Sam's eyes widened as it dawned on him that his hostages had a cavalry coming for them. It was some sort of distress signal. A GPS leading straight to their location. He tried his best to remain calm. "And just why the hell would you tell me about this? Why would you show this?"

Roland smiled, rolling his sleeve back over the watch. He

sat back comfortably like he no longer had any cares in the world, despite the gun still aimed at him.

"Why?" He yawned. "Because at this point, there's absolutely nothing you can do about it. It's too late for you to do a damn thing. Even if you killed us, broke the bracelet, they're already close. They'll be here any minute."

Roland fastened his seat belt and Ulrich did the same up front, winking at Sam in the rear view mirror. "I would buckle up if I were you."

Almost on cue, there was a pop—a sudden blast of air—and he knew that at least one of the car's tires had burst. Sam quickly pulled down the strap of his seat belt and clicked it in place, just in the nick of time. The car weaved and wobbled uneasily, tilting about on the road. Ulrich didn't seem to be bothered at the wheel by the disturbance. There was another pop and another tire gave out beneath the vehicle.

The car suddenly careened hard and flipped over completely, its roof skidding across the road before coming to a halt in the grass nearby. All of its passengers would have been thrown about the car if not for the seat belts strapped over their bodies, causing them all to instead stay suspended upside down in their seats, reeling from the whiplash of the crash.

Sam's whole body ached but he was glad to still be breathing. He opened his eyes but found himself in a disorienting world, hanging upside down where he sat. Blood rushed down into his head and he felt thankful that he was at least buckled in. That was kind of Roland to suggest that he put it on before the crash. Roland may have been a member of an evil secret society but at least he cared about safe driving.

Sam let out a groan and craned his head to the seat beside him. Roland was recovering from the crash too. Sam noticed that the pistol he had was now beneath him on the flipped ceiling of the car. He must have dropped it during all of the commotion, and without it, he lost the only bit of leverage he had.

Roland, still struggling to recover himself, also took notice of the firearm on the ceiling between them. They both stared at the pistol and then looked at each other. The same thought crossed their minds at the same moment— get that weapon.

Both of them reached out for it but it was just beyond how far their arms could stretch. Their fingertips were only an inch away from the grip. That small of a margin might make the difference between life and death. Roland released a frustrated growl and tried to unbuckle his seat belt but was having trouble with it. Thankfully, the strap seemed to have been damaged during the crash.

Feeling trapped and unable to get out, Roland instead focused his energy on hitting Sam to stop him from unbuckling himself. Sam blocked his punches and returned a few of his own, and the two traded blows while hanging upside down. From where they sat, stuck beside each other, it wouldn't take long for one to beat the other to death, and Sam knew that he wouldn't be on the winning side of a brawl like that.

He let Roland land a couple of blows and focused on shifting his energy to get loose. He tried to click his seat belt, but it seemed jammed up from the crash just like Roland's. While that seat belt might have saved his life when the car flipped, now it might be the death of him, keeping him from escape while he was brutally beaten to death. It was the worst possible time for his buckle to not be working properly. He pulled at the strap hard with one hand while trying to block Roland's strikes with the other.

Finally, after yanking as hard as he could, the strap came loose and away from his body. The seat belt came undone, dropping him down hard from where he was suspended, head first onto the car's ceiling.

At least now he could reach the gun. It hurt to move but he managed to grab the pistol, and part of him considered using it on the two Black Sun agents while they were stuck, but he couldn't bring himself to do it. He wouldn't kill someone so defenseless like that. They may have been trying to abduct him, but they hadn't tried to kill him. He wouldn't kill them when they weren't at least intending to do the same to him.

He started painfully crawling toward the door on his side of the car, away from the upside down Roland, who still flailed and thrashed around helplessly from where he was hanging in the car seat. He tried reaching for Sam, as

Sam pushed the car door open to escape and crawled out of the overturned vehicle.

As he pulled himself out into the fresh air and the mud, Sam felt impossibly shaky. He was still disoriented from the force of the car flipping, but at least he was moving. Once he was completely out of the car, he tried his best to get to his feet. His whole equilibrium felt off balance, and it hurt to stand, but he forced himself up.

Once he was standing firmly enough that he didn't feel like he was about to tip, he turned back to the overturned car. Both tires on its left side had been completely destroyed, popped like balloons. The rubber was just hanging loosely over the metal wheels.

Both Black Sun operatives were slowly pulling themselves from the wreckage just like he had. Sam had kind of hoped Roland would stay stuck in his seat but he knew he wasn't that lucky. Ulrich must have been able to help Roland out of his buckle, because they both emerged from the vehicle and started limping unsteadily toward him. Ulrich looked like he caught the brunt of the crash; a large, bloody gash ran down his face from a deep wound over his brow. Maybe his air bag hadn't deployed.

Both of them winced as they moved, looking like they were doing their best to ignore the pain that came with each little step they took. Whatever reinforcements had come and flipped the car had done quite a number on their own allies. Sam wasn't really surprised; he doubted the Black Sun cared if their own men died, as long as the overall task was completed.

Sam tried to get away but he wasn't moving very well either. He was close to collapsing. The whole world around him was spinning. He tightened his grip on the pistol in his hand and pointed it at his wounded enemies. This might be his only chance. Shooting the two of them might be the only chance he had at getting away.

Ulrich and Roland saw the gun pointed their way and both stopped their pursuit.

"Last chance to get the hell away from me," Sam said.

The two men looked at one another for a moment and then back at Sam, slowly starting their approach again, one step at a time. His threat had slid off of them like it was nothing more than simple words ... maybe that was really all it was.

"We can't do that," Ulrich said, wiping away some of the blood on his check. "We have our orders. We're taking you to Corvus, whether you like it or not."

"No," Sam said. He waved the gun to remind them who had the upper hand. "I respectfully decline. That's not going to happen."

"Then you will have to shoot us!" Roland snapped, holding out his arms like he was awaiting the bullets to come any minute, like he welcomed them. "You keep pointing that at our faces but I don't think you're going to pull the trigger, are you? It doesn't look like it to me."

"He's not," a female voice came from behind Sam.

He turned around to find the source of those words—

Sasha was standing there, a sniper rifle at her side. She looked from Sam to her fellow Black Sun agents, then back to Sam again, with that smug expression that Sam remembered from when he first met her in Jerusalem. She was an enforcer, a soldier, and a murderer, loyally serving the Order of the Black Sun, even when she was under the command of a psychopath like Julian Corvus.

"Sam Cleave is not going to just gun down two men in the middle of the road. Not these days, at least. Isn't that right, Sam?"

"Sasha..." He was too stunned by her sudden appearance to offer an intelligent response. He looked around her to see if there were any vehicles nearby. There was nothing but the possible shape of a car a long way across the valley. She had got here first and walked all that way, just to set a trap for Sam, just to free her allies.

Sasha dropped her sniper rifle and took a step closer, still smiling. "It's been some time since we last saw each other, hasn't it? Since looking for the Spear of Destiny. Back in the swamp cave in Norwich."

"Yeah..." Sam said uneasily. He remembered it very well. What he remembered most was how much he didn't like her. She was nothing more than hired muscle for the Black Sun to use as a blunt instrument. A cold killer who only knew how to be a weapon, and nothing else. "Yeah I remember. You went running for the hills when Julian Corvus fell into that pit. From what I have heard, his luck has more than improved since that tumble he took."

Sam aimed his gun at Sasha now. She wasn't injured like her two comrades, and despite dropping the sniper rifle, she still had a weapon within her reach. She was groomed to be a killer and could easily take out Sam if it came to it, unarmed or not. Most importantly, Sam knew the truth about his three enemies. He knew full well that Sasha was the leader and the most dangerous of the trio he was up against.

"You blew out the tires," he said through gritted teeth. "You could have killed us."

"I know," she said with a simple shrug of her shoulders.

"You're cold," Sam grimaced. "Were you there when Purdue got burned alive?"

Sasha nodded. "I was. In fact, if you really want to know, I was the very last person who saw Purdue that night."

"So you came to finish me off too? Or are you here to help these morons bring me to your boss?"

Sasha again looked hard at Sam and then shifted her gaze behind him to Ulrich and Roland. They were inching slowly toward Sam from behind, probably hoping to jump him while he was distracted by Sasha's arrival. Sasha brought her attention back to Sam. He was still pointing his gun at her head.

"I'm going to ask nicely that you stop trying to put up a fight. It won't make any difference from here on out, because no matter how much you resist, I am taking you from here," Sasha said. Something strange crossed her face and Sam couldn't place it. "But not to Julian."

There was confusion behind Sam. Ulrich and Roland stopped in their tracks and stared at Sasha with uncertainty. They looked flabbergasted by the decision she was making. Sam shared their confusion. If he wasn't being taken to Julian Corvus, then where could Sasha be planning on taking him?

Ulrich's face grew red and all of his anger that had been fixated on Purdue shifted to Sasha. "What the hell are you talking about, woman?! Of course he's going to Julian! We have our ord—"

Sasha suddenly drew a pistol from her belt, in one stunningly fast motion, and fired just as quickly. If she had been going after Sam, he would have been dead long before he had a chance to fire his own weapon. As it turned out, though, Sasha wasn't targeting Sam. She had other targets in mind to kill.

Two shots rang out and both bullets flew past Sam's head. Ulrich and Roland collapsed, each with a bullet planted perfectly between their eyes. They were both dead immediately, the second the bullets entered beneath their brows. They would never be able to hunt anyone down ever again.

Sam had the instinctive urge to return fire but was frozen in place from shock, too stunned to even try. None of what was happening made any sense to him. It was like he was watching a movie that had taken a major twist, and all he could do was sit in the audience and be baffled that it was unfolding before him.

"Don't just stand there, you moron. Come with me. Now."

He didn't have any other choice. He could stay in the middle of nowhere with a flipped over car and two dead bodies. He could try his luck of picking a direction and walking to find any sort of civilization; maybe he would follow the road back to some place far less deserted than his current location. Or he could follow a woman who he knew was his enemy, who had been since the moment they first met.

Sam settled on the latter of his options.

Sam tried to keep up with Sasha as they walked through the field of grass toward the car in the distance, but she was a brisk walker, and didn't even bother looking back to see if he was still following. Sam glanced back and could still see the overturned vehicle and the bodies beside it. The carnage left in the wake of whatever was going through Sasha's mind; by whatever caused her to fight members of her own group.

"What the hell was that back there?!" Sam called ahead. "What was that?!"

She didn't answer and just kept walking. He was still holding the pistol in his hand, and still wasn't sure if he should be using it or not. She could be leading him somewhere worse than Ulrich and Roland were taking him. Hell, she could be hand delivering him to Julian Corvus himself as some special favor or as a way of earning the new Black Sun leader's favor.

He tried to think of any possible reasons she would want to save him, and even go so far as killing her own men to see it through. Nothing sprang to mind. She didn't owe him anything. His life certainly shouldn't have mattered more than the lives of her own men.

Sasha protected him, and murdered members of the Black Sun to do it.

Why?

"Those were your friends," Sam said in bewilderment. "Those were you friends and you gunned them down without a second thought. There wasn't any hesitation at all. Hell, I would say you really wanted to do it ... maybe even were waiting for the chance."

"They weren't my friends," Sasha said matter of factly, still maintaining her hasty pace through the field.

"Fine," Sam said and rolled his eyes. "You shot up your coworkers and colleagues then. Better? Why would you do that? Isn't the Order of the Black Sun going to have to ... I don't know ... punish you or something for that? Aren't they going to be mad?"

"What are you doing?" Sasha balked. "You trying to

conduct an interview for one of your big stories, Sam? You trying to use me as your big scoop?"

"No story, though this would make for one hell of a head-line," Sam said. "I'm just trying to wrap my head around how someone could do that. Something so callous..."

"What are you complaining about?" Sasha raised her voice and yelled into the air, letting the breeze take her anger back to the man following her, rather than turn and look him in the eyes. "All you're doing is whining. All you need to know is that I saved your ungrateful little ass. If they brought you to Julian, how do you think that would have turned out for you?"

Sam remembered the pale eyes of Julian Corvus well. That man was unhinged and crueler than most people Sam had met, maybe even most people on the entire planet. The Order of the Black Sun was bad enough before, but with Julian reigning over them, large and in charge, things could only be getting much, much worse since his induction. Whatever Julian had done to take over leadership of the entire order, it couldn't have been good. If anything, it was something horrific, because he knew that Julian relished that kind of murderous environment.

If Sam was brought to Julian, he would probably be killed in some terrible and excessively gruesome fashion. Or if he became Julian's prisoner, Sam might even be allowed to live but have to suffer torture every day for the slights against Julian that Sam had helped Purdue and Nina make.

Sam didn't like Sasha very much and he never had. She was a cold, homicidal enforcer for a group that obviously wasn't on the right side. Despite her tough outer shell, Sasha wasn't nearly as demented and plagued by demons as Julian. Sasha even seemed afraid of Julian back when they were all looking for the Spear of Destiny together.

"If I was in front of Julian Corvus again ... well. I will just stick to this. It probably wouldn't end well for me. Not at all."

"Exactly," Sasha said. "And if we're going to bring down Julian, we're going to need all the numbers we can get. All of them."

They approached the lone car parked in the grass, and it was indeed the vehicle Sasha used to come ambush Ulrich and Roland. She started unlocking the car, but Sam barely noticed the automobile. At that moment, all he could think about was images of Julian finally being taken down a peg or two, and looking up at them with both anger and acceptance. He wanted that so badly. He needed to prove that he could beat Julian, but at this moment time, there was no way he could accomplish that on his own.

"Bring down Julian?"

"That's what I said," Sasha said. "He's tearing apart the order. Defiling it with all of his horrors. Ruining the Order of the Black Sun by taking it down a path it should never have gone. His ascension was never supposed to happen. It shouldn't have. I couldn't stop it from happening back then but maybe I mean to correct that. I can and I will."

Sasha didn't sound like the blood thirsty mercenary he met in Jerusalem, and she certainly didn't sound like the loyal Julian Corvus supporter that she had played in Norwich. She didn't seem like a follower anymore. Now she was more confident and seemed more comfortable in her own skin. She was something entirely else than he remembered.

He might have even been impressed, because he found himself asking her questions about her intentions and the means of seeing them through. "Do you have any help? Any other Black Sun members who are standing beside you against him?"

"None," Sasha said. "And I can't risk even trying to recruit anyone. Far too many of them are loyal to Julian and those tendrils of his are wrapped around so many of their minds. They're not thinking straight. They're just seeing the grand promises he makes about spreading our influence over all aspects of the future, about making the order more powerful than we've ever been. They're all falling for his lies and his empty assurances. He's corrupting the Order of the Black Sun from the inside."

Sam wanted to argue that the Order of the Black Sun was already corrupt and had been for a long, long time, but he kept quiet. He was not in the mood to get into a pointless debate, not when he was still trying to just process everything that was happening. The last few minutes were still a dizzying flurry of abnormal events, or maybe that was just his splitting headache from the car flip affecting him.

Sasha continued. "So I've been bringing together help from outside of the order, from people who might be able to put up a fight against Julian Corvus. Some even have personal reasons for wanting him to be taken down."

"Gee, if only we had David Purdue right about now," Sam said vindictively, his words laced with hatred toward the ones that took his friend away. "If only he hadn't been burned alive in his own home."

"My thoughts exactly," Sasha said after ignoring Sam's spiteful tone. She opened her car door to get in but remained standing outside. "Which is why Purdue is going to be the biggest asset we will have at our disposal during all of this."

Sam was starting to get angry. It didn't matter how she claimed Purdue was going to be an asset. He wasn't going to be anything helpful as a pile of ash. Addressing Purdue like he was still around was insulting, especially when it was coming from someone who had a hand in his death. She was speaking about him like all of that fiery death hadn't happened, and there wasn't even a hint of guilt in her voice. She didn't seem at all phased that she was part of the reason he was gone.

He hated that Sasha was apparently the last person to see Purdue alive, and probably the last face Purdue saw before his world was burned around him. Purdue deserved a better final view than that. He deserved a longer life and a less painful death.

Sam let his simmering rage out of himself. "So you're going to what...? Going to use David Purdue's memory to further your cause? Make him a martyr? A symbol of how bad the Order of the Black Sun has become so you can take over as leader of the goddamn hive of monsters? Purdue would never have wanted his name used like that. If he was alive, he wouldn't have wanted any part of it. He, Nina, and I would have had nothing to do with Black Sun infighting that would decide which winner was going to screw us over next. He would have had none of it!"

"On the contrary, Purdue is more than willing to help remove Julian by whatever means necessary. He wants retribution on Julian for taking everything from him. That's the only thing that's keeping him going ... besides, of course, that the Black Sun has Dr. Nina Gould and Purdue's butler as prisoners. He wants to rescue them while resolving the grudge that nearly got him killed. In fact, from what I've seen, Purdue is taking steps to do just that this very moment."

"Why are you talking about him like he's still here?? He's not! Purdue is dead! He's gone! The Order of the Black Sun, Julian Corvus, even you ... all of you bastards saw to that! You all killed him!"

Sasha shook her head. "You're wrong. You want to know what I saw to? What I am responsible for? I made sure Purdue didn't get incinerated. I saw to seeing him safe. I even dragged him out of that burning house."

An image of that scenario, of her description of her supposed action, flashed in Sam's head and it gave him a headache just to try and imagine it. That was one of the most ridiculous things Sam could try to imagine. It was ludicrous. There was no reason why Sasha would save Purdue ... although, he would have thought the same thing about himself, but here Sasha was, having murdered her own team to make sure Sam survived. If she could do something like that ... was it possible that she helped Purdue as well after all? It just didn't seem real. It didn't seem possible in any sort of universe, under any circumstances.

"What...?" Sam still tried to picture it. He stared at her hard, trying to find some sign that she was playing him, some evidence that she was lying to his face. There was nothing. She looked so serious. If she was lying, she was unbelievably good at it. If her expression didn't give away the truth, he would have to see if she could lie verbally as well as she could look convincing. "What are you ... what are you saying exactly? What the hell are you...?"

He couldn't even finish his last question. He was breathing so heavily that the air was practically muting his own voice. The possibility of his friend's survival was sapping all of his energy. He was completely over-whelmed by the spark of hope growing in him, mixed with the high chance that all of this was nothing more than a lie she concocted.

Sasha just stared at him in silence, letting him try and catch his own breath. She was probably enjoying the conflict he was having with himself, probably relishing every second he was suffering from not knowing if her claims were real.

He'd had enough of her tormenting him. He just needed the relief of knowing the truth.

"WHAT ARE YOU SAYING!?"

"I'm telling you that David Purdue was not killed that night," Sasha said. "He didn't die in that fire. He didn't even catch on fire. And as far as I know, he's still alive this very moment."

Sam's mind was racing. He wanted more answers and details. It was like he was back in the backseat listening to his captors recap Purdue's final moments, but this time, he wasn't listening to a sad story about the specifics of his friend's death. Now he was hearing a similar story but with a far different ending ... an ending that could change everything.

"I don't ... are you serious?"

"I am," Sasha said. The way she looked at him was different than she ever had before. There wasn't anything malicious behind her face. It seemed sincere—no—it was sincere. He knew it now. He knew Sasha was telling him the truth. "Happy? So hurry up and get in the car. We have work to do."

Sasha got into the driver's seat and Sam unsteadily went

around the hood and got in the passenger seat beside her. They took off, getting back onto the road. Again, he was in a car with a member of the Black Sun, driving to some unknown destination. This time, though, he wasn't trying to figure out his own survival, he was trying to figure out his friend's survival.

Sam had so many questions but those could wait. He needed a moment to exhale, and release all of the stress he had been feeling since he'd been on the run, since Purdue called him and warned him to flee from the Black Sun. For the first time since that phone call, Sam actually felt some comfort and happiness.

Wherever he was, David Purdue was alive.

7

THE IMPORTANCE OF THE LETTER X

Purdue looked over the items they had stolen from the museum; all of Admiral Ogden's belongings that had been swallowed by the sea. He laid everything out on the table in his quarters. The barnacle encrusted cutlass. The flintlock pistol that had been smoothed out into driftwood. To think, at one point that sword and that pistol were used to kill and plunder. Who knew how many people's blood had the stained the now brittle blade of the cutlass? Or how many shots had been fried from that flintlock and found their mark? All of these items were the remnants of a man's violent history.

He laid out the map beside it all. It was strange. There was a time, centuries ago, that the famed pirate had probably sat in his own private quarters and had his sword and pistol by his side, charting the map that would lead to his prizes. Now, long after he was gone, those same items were together again, in the hands of an explorer. If Admiral Ogden ever imagined who might find his treasure someday, Purdue hoped that he was worthy of whatever person the pirate had concocted in his imagination.

Purdue rolled the map open to look at all of those Xs strewn about the old parchment again, just like he did every day. He then looked over the old misshapen piece of wood that was once a functioning pistol. Somehow, that old waterlogged pistol was supposed to help figure out the map. He had no idea how, but there was only one way to find out. The map lay before him with its dozens of X's and he looked them over with the same fervor he always did. Each time he'd given the map an inspection, he hoped he would see something that would give him some sort of hint. Now that he had the other items, maybe he would finally see something new.

He could have asked some of the crew for assistance, and maybe he would still consider it if he kept getting stumped. But he would prefer finding the secret of the map on his own. It would be safer if he was the only one who knew how to decipher it. Otherwise, he might not be needed by them anymore and be tossed in the ocean by the twins, just like that policeman had been.

So he kept his door locked while he looked at the belongings. He appreciated the peace and quiet. Spending so much time cramped on a boat with a bunch of strangers was exhausting.

On the flintlock, there were a number of Xs carved into

the smoothed out wood. Most of the markings were faded from the damage done by its time on the ocean floor, but they were still there if you looked close enough.

Most who examined the pistol probably thought the Xs represented a kill, a tally of everyone Admiral Ogden had gunned down over his years of plundering. Those people would be wrong to think that. They didn't have the map like he did. With it, he could see the bigger picture. He could see that the Xs on the charts corresponded with the same markings on the gun. The placements of each X were identical, spaced perfectly according to the map.

As he looked back and forth, taking note of each matching mark, he found one striking difference—an X on the flintlock was missing.

There was an extra one on the map right on top of a little island off the coast of Venezuela. He didn't recognize the land mass but it looked miniscule in comparison to even the smaller islands around it. It was barely even visible over the X that was drawn over it.

He double checked the flintlock carefully. That X could have been covered by the wood being smoothed out but he doubted it. One had never been carved. Everything else matched so perfectly. It couldn't have been a mistake. It couldn't have.

That little island on the map was important, maybe even where Admiral Ogden's treasure was. If you were just looking at the map alone, you would be overwhelmed by all of the Xs. There would be no way of knowing which one—or if any at all—was pointing out the real location. With the flintlock's help, you could see through all of the decoys and distractions. It was ingenious. Admiral Ogden probably never went anywhere without his pistol. Hell he probably died with it in his hand or tucked into his belt. A perfect key to have for the truth of his spoils.

The missing X was the important one. In this case, it wasn't X that marked the spot; it was its absence.

That island across the Caribbean Sea was their next destination. He had no doubt about that.

Now he just needed to decide how he was going to present the information to the crew. How much could he disclose without risking becoming expendable to them? Sure, they seemed to be working well but he didn't even remotely trust them. At best they were a group of scoundrels loyal to whoever paid them. At worst, they were all as bad as the twins and just waiting for a chance to turn on him. He would need to tread very carefully with how he was going to proceed with the crew.

Even after he figured out the riddle of the flintlock, he waited for some time in the fragile security of his private quarters. When he finally emerged back out onto the deck, many of the crew were beaming with enthusiasm and excited to see him.

"How did it go? Alton asked with a big, friendly smile. It was like their last discussion hadn't been a contentious one at all; even though Alton had tried to embarrass Purdue's leadership in front of the whole crew. Now they were suddenly supposed to be best friends. "Did you find what you were looking for?"

"Aye, I hope so," Purdue said. "Though it's hardly a guarantee. At least we have a heading. We'll see what we see when we get there."

He looked out at the water stretching out into the horizon. Hopefully they were on their way to the treasure and toward reclaiming his life from the ones who took it from him. They had their coordinates but he wouldn't share anything beyond that; like how he found the location. There was a still a good chance that he was mistaken and the missing X on the map wasn't important at all. They could very well be heading to a dead end.

Something kept telling him not to worry though. All he had was a feeling in his gut that the little island on the map was the right place. That was all he had to go on, and it would have to be enough.

There was an excitement permeating the ship. The crew's attitude was growing more positive now that they had an actual destination the ship was going toward. There was a sentiment that their efforts were finally going to be rewarded, and that the prize they were seeking wasn't hypothetical or part of some fable anymore.

They all were starting to believe that they were going to

get the treasure. They were going to be rich. They were all going to have a chance to please their dangerous boss who they all feared so much. Their status would be heightened after this voyage.

"You look worried," Alton snickered as Purdue looked out at the waves.

"Not worried," Purdue said. "Just hoping for the best. Wouldn't want this to be a pointless detour, now would we?"

"No," Alton admitted. "The Wharf Man wants this to go as ... as smoothly as possible."

Every time Alton spoke, the lingering shadow of the Wharf Man loomed close behind him. His loyalty was very apparent and he always made sure to remind people of the monstrous crime lord that was supporting him and his actions.

Purdue turned to face Alton. "Satiate my curiosity for a moment. What's the story with you and your boss? The Wharf Man obviously thinks highly of you. He trusts you. You're his eyes. You're his ears."

"His will," Alton added proudly.

"Exactly," Purdue said. "Not to pry, but how the hell did that come about? Must take a lot to be respected so much by a man like that."

Alton looked out at the water and his usual confidence slipped off his face. Whatever memories were passing through his head, they weren't pleasant. Maybe he hadn't thought back so far in a long time. It all washed over him quickly and then fell away, and his bright smile returned to his face.

"You want to know why I am so loved, hmm? Simple. I did as I was told. I followed the rules. I earned everything that he has given me. Hard work, you know? Hard work. I won the Wharf Man's trust."

"And your brother too?"

"Of course," Alton laughed. "That is why we are here."

"But the Wharf Man ripped out his tongue—"

"Oniel did that to himself. The Wharf Man may have been the one to pull it from his mouth, but it was my brother's mistake." Alton acted like the mutilation was the most justifiable thing in the world. Like he was defending someone whose actions were saving the entire world.

They both glanced across the deck where Oniel lingered, silently observing the rest of the crew like he always did.

Alton continued, "My brother always had a sharp tongue. It got him into trouble many times. He is better off without it ... and he has learned his lesson to never speak out of line again."

"He doesn't have much of a choice now," Purdue muttered under his breath.

"My brother and I could only settle for scraps before.

138

The Wharf Man helped us. Got us off of the streets, and gave us a purpose. We all need purpose, do we not?"

Purdue couldn't argue with him there.

"Like you," Alton said. "Your purpose is to get your money back, no? And so you have come to us for help. It was a good choice. The Wharf Man is a good friend to have on your side, especially when you need him most. You play well together, and he might even help you take back what is yours from those thieves who took it from you."

Purdue brightened a little at the prospect. A powerful crime syndicate backing him would be undeniably helpful against the Order of the Black Sun. Even when he got Admiral Ogden's treasure and replenished some of his fortune, he would still just be one man against an expansive secret society. He wouldn't be able to do much good on his own. With the Wharf Man supporting him, he could maybe stand up to the Black Sun. They could be the deciding factor in all of this.

Then again, getting in bed with a crime kingpin was a risky choice, but he'd long since run out of good possible choices to make. Maybe he could use the extra muscle.

"Maybe," Purdue said honestly. "We'll see how this all turns out, aye?"

"Of course," Alton said with a grin. "Between you and me, my friend, we could do with a good fight. Especially if it means fighting for a friend."

Purdue didn't quite consider a murderous man like Alton a friend, but he took the meaning. And maybe a friend like Alton, his brother, and their superior would be the exact kind of allies Purdue needed at this point in time. They were already helping him with this, what harm was there in working together a short time longer once they were finished finding the treasure?

Besides, he didn't exactly have a lot of friends anymore.

Admiral Ogden stood on the port side railing of the docked *Scarlet Wing*, looking out to the sea. His crew was hard at work behind him on the deck, carrying supplies on board that would last them through their next few months at sea, for all of their countless raids they were going to be launching on other vessels. He was hopeful for those days ahead and would often daydream about the potential amount of valuables they could add to his enormous stockpile. While any of those victories would be good, he wanted to win a large prize; something that would exponentially increase his already impressive amount of riches.

And thankfully, that kind of venture came running right up to him on the deck. One of the deckhands, Gregory sprinted up the gangplank and practically threw himself onto his commanding officer. He was out of breath and filled to the brim with excitement.

"I come with news, Admiral," he said through gasps. "Very good news."

"Spit it out then."

Whatever it was, Gregory seemed happy about it, and even happier that he was the one to be giving the good news.

"Captain Brown and Captain Fallon have sent word of a massive Spanish galleon coming across the Atlantic."

"And how is it that they acquired this information?"

"They were part of a raid near Spain and brought down a warship. And that's the best part, Admiral. They managed to get the transport's schedule. We know exactly where that gold is going to be and when."

The potential of that prize danced across Admiral Ogden's face. A cache like that would be a great target to hit and an even better trophy to add to their collection. Best of all, with its schedule, they would have the means to plan a perfect ambush.

It was far too large of a job for one ship, though. Even two ships would be risky and three would still be difficult. No, they would need the full might of his power to bring to bear. As many of his fleet that he could amass.

"Send word out to all of the captains, it doesn't matter what bloody ocean they're in right now. We'll need them. As many as we can muster for this."

Gregory looked a bit bewildered by the decision. It had

been some time since the fleet came together as one functioning unit. It would surely be a sight to behold. He nodded dutifully, but looked rather anxious as he set out to complete his task.

The galleon didn't seem to know how to respond to the dozen ships that descended upon it. It was surrounded before it even had the chance to try to flee. It was well armed, as expected, given the contents of its cargo, and would have been able to handle up to maybe three of their ships with ease, but it wasn't ready to take on an entire fleet of pirates by itself.

Admiral Ogden gave his ships strict orders not to sink the galleon, even if it did try to put up a fight. They couldn't risk losing that gold to the currents. They would have to board and capture the ship and plunder its cache.

Once their blockade was cemented, a white flag of surrender waved above the galleon. Ogden brought the *Scarlet Wing* closer, its red canvas leading the assault. Once they were close, Ogden took a number of longboats as part of a boarding party. Just to be safe, other members of their fleet sent their own longboats to aid in the takeover.

The Spanish galleon was swarmed by pirates rowing toward it. They may have surrendered but Ogden had fallen victim to ploys like that in the past. A white flag to lure attackers in with their guards down and full of confidence, primed to fall prey to a trap. He wouldn't make that mistake. As they approached, he eyed the galleon's cannons carefully. The Spanish could easily open fire on the encroaching rowboats. They would be far easier to face than the fleet itself.

The crew made their way up to the galleon's deck. Admiral Ogden drew his cutlass; if there was a fight waiting for them on the deck, he was going to be ready for it. When they pulled themselves onto the galleon, he found the galleon's crew facing them, but they didn't have their weapons drawn. They were on their knees, with their hands on the deck. They really had surrendered. None of the Spaniards even spoke. They just kept their heads down.

"Not putting up a fight," Ogden said to one of them. "You made a very wise decision. Stay right where you are and we will be on our way in no time at all."

Ogden led a group below deck to the cargo hold. He kicked the door open and entered a room filled to the brim with boxes and chests. It was an incredible sight and he relished that this would be one of their biggest successes to date. Surprisingly, it hadn't been as much of a challenge as he expected, but it did make things easier to have a loyal armada at your back.

Victorious, he opened up one of the closest chests—it was empty.

He opened up the one beside it and it was just as hollow. He whistled and the men he brought below deck got to work prying open the crates and chests. It took some time but they found themselves no richer than they had been when they came inside. All of the chests were empty. There was no gold.

Then what the hell was the galleon doing? Had the gold already been delivered? No. No, if it had, there wouldn't be any chests on board. It was transporting nothing of any value at all.

There was a whistling and he could hear cannon fire somewhere outside.

"Upstairs! Now!"

When Ogden got back on deck, he found a battle raging in the waters around them. Royal navy warships had appeared and flanked his fleet's ships. They must have been hidden around the ben of the island's shoreline, out of view.

This was a trap. It was all a trap, and he had sailed right into it. There had never been any gold being transported. It had just been shiny bait, and Ogden swam after it without a second thought. He should have been smarter than that. He knew it had been too easy but never questioned it. Damn his greed; and the shine of potentially vast amounts of gold for blinding him to what should have been obvious.

He looked down at the prisoners who weren't acting like prisoners at all anymore. They were smiling now, probably embracing the role they had gotten to play in the surprise attack. Ogden wanted to execute them all on the spot, but there were bigger concerns.

The blockade of vessels his fleet formed was quickly falling apart. Taken by surprise by the British armada, many of the ships were being blown apart by cannonballs on fire. Some even turned their ships around in hopes of escape but were immediately bombarded before they could sail away. Even the *Scarlet Wing* was being pelted by enemy fire.

Admiral Ogden was helpless to protect the fleet he'd built. He couldn't stop the vessels from being overrun, decimated, and swallowed by the sea.

Only one of his ships remained undamaged. The *Iron Horn*, captained by his old first mate, Jacob Morrow. It had miraculously avoided being hit by any enemy. Strangely, the naval vessels didn't seem to be targeting the *Iron Horn* at all. No cannonballs splashed anywhere near it, in any direction. They were treating Morrow's vessel like it was one of their own—maybe it was.

That troubling thought clawed into Ogden's head and planted itself there. That was it. All of this had been orchestrated by Morrow. One of his most trusted allies had betrayed him.

The *Iron Horn* came beside the galleon. Some of the men at Ogden's side celebrated its arrival, thinking it was a rescue and that Morrow would ferry them to safety, but Ogden could see the truth. He could see it so clearly. The

Iron Horn's sails were being carried by the winds of treachery.

When he looked at the ship's deck, Morrow's expression confirmed the theories that were frantically bouncing in his head. Morrow looked elated, happier than Ogden had seen him look in years. And when his crew threw down planks between the ships and started boarding the galleon, the men beside Ogden hoping for a rescue quickly learned the truth when their former comrades started cutting them down one-by-one.

A fight broke out as Ogden's boarding party tried to defend themselves. The admiral half-heartily jointed the brawl, but felt a crippling sense of dread come over him as he fought. What did it matter to fight back? His legendary pirate fleet was obliterated. The men under his command were being slaughtered. Even if he killed Morrow and his crew for turning on him, there was a still a fleet of British vessels to contend with. He couldn't hope to defeat them. He wouldn't stand a chance.

Captain Morrow himself crossed the plank to the galleon and entered the fray, sword in hand. He sliced and stabbed his way through the crowd, coming for Ogden.

Despite the despair sweeping over him, Ogden welcomed the chance to run his sword through Morrow. If this was indeed going to be Admiral Ogden's final battle, he would make sure that traitor was dead before he fell.

Morrow had always been a capable swordsman but Ogden knew he could best him in a proper duel. Unfortunately, Morrow didn't seem interested in a proper duel at all. Once he was closing in on Ogden, he drew his pistol from his belt and fired a shot into the admirals leg. Ogden's body buckled beneath him and he fell to one knee. Morrow brought his cutlass down, but even injured, Ogden held him at bay with his own weapon. He had to even the playing field or he was going to be killed.

He waited until Morrow took another swing and when their swords clashed, Ogden took hold of Morrow's wrist and pulled him down to the deck. The two men grappled and wrestled about while the rest of the deck was filled with the sounds of screams and clattering metal. It was far from a traditional duel, but if Morrow wanted a rougher fight, then Ogden would be sure that it was exactly what he received.

After a brief but intense struggle, Ogden overpowered Morrow. He wrapped his fingers around Morrow's throat, ready to wring his neck. All of that confidence and pride that Morrow showed during his betrayal washed away, replaced by horror at the realization that he was going to lose.

"Help! Help!" Morrow gasped out. "Get this bastard off of me!"

Ogden squeezed his neck harder, hoping to silence him. It was no use, though, as his pleas were heard by his crew and some of the navy soldiers coming on board the galleon. Something hard struck Ogden on the back of the head and he fell to his stomach in a daze. Morrow slowly got to his feet as two men heaved Ogden up and restrained him.

"You always were a lecherous little shit, weren't you?" Ogden groaned. "I knew that already, of course, but never thought that you would throw your hat in with England. It didn't think you were that much of a coward. You couldn't just face me yourself. You had to go crawling to the crown and beg them for help. You damn child. So, you're what ... enlisted as a proud member of the royal navy now?"

"Privateer, actually," Morrow said, his smugness returning now that he was out of harm's way and in control. "I told you that we should be trying to increase our station in life. Now I get to be a pirate legally."

"Not a pirate at all then," Ogden said coldly. "A government dog. That's all. All because I wouldn't give up and waste the gold like you wanted me to."

"With that many men, that many ships, I couldn't exactly put together a mutiny, could I? It would have been incredibly foolish. That fire would have been snuffed out before it began. I'm no fool."

Ogden laughed, not at all convinced of that.

"You can mock me all you want. It was the most intelligent move to make," Morrow said with a shrug. "As one man with a handful of supporters, I wouldn't have stood a chance against the great pirate fleet of Walton Ogden. But as a privateer ... as a privateer with intimate knowledge of that fleet, the crown backs me happily. Better to be an asset to them than a tool to help you needlessly throw our lives away in search of needless wealth."

"That's it then?" Ogden asked, forcing a smile. "You paint yourself as a genius tactician, when in truth you're just a traitorous leech that has thrown away all trust we ever put in you. Look around you. These people were your crew. Your family once. Jacob ... we were friends."

"Were we?" Morrow glanced around at the bodies on deck and the burning ships across the water. "I imagine friends would share the spoils that they both helped to earn. Instead, you have hoarded our collected treasure in some undisclosed location and kept it all for yourself. That belonged to all of us. Not just you. The other captains in the fleet might have been content with letting you decided what to do with the treasure, but I wasn't."

"Clearly," Ogden said sharply. "You never were easy to please were you?"

"And you were never satisfied, no matter how much coin you put in your pocket. I'm done letting your insatiable greed put my life at risk."

"Well..." Ogden leaned forward as much as he could. "You've obviously made your decision. Go on then. Tell your men to get their grubby little hands off me and let's finish this right here and now."

"Finish?" Morrow chuckled. "You're mistaken, Walton. This is just the beginning. We have dealt these ships of yours a large blow. And with you defeated, your remaining legion of pirates won't be much trouble at all. I told you, I know the inner workings of your armada better than anyone else. I know your ships and your crew, their strategies, and their routines. As we speak, we have dispatched ships to clear up the remaining ships that you have patrolling the waters for more victims. The few remaining that you didn't call to plunder this galleon or were too far away. That's the problem with having such a large force under the complete control of one man. You spread yourself thin, or group everyone to close together. We'll destroy everyone here, and then put holes in whatever ships you have left. They will sink to the ocean floor. Just like your flagship."

Ogden looked past Morrow at the red sails of the *Scarlet Wing*. It was on fire, clearly taking on water from the number of holes in the hull.

"I will kill you for this," Ogden said.

"No. No, I don't think you will."

Morrow followed his gaze to the ship they once sailed on together. He looked back and smiled, pointing his sword at the flagship.

"It is customary for the captain to go down with the ship, is it not? But, as you just love to point out all the time, you're not a captain anymore, are you, Walton? No, you're beyond that now, right? You're an admiral of an entire armada of vessels now. So you don't get the captain's privilege of joining your ship to the bottom of the sea. You'll just have to settle for watching."

Ogden tried to pull himself from the grip of the soldiers

but they easily restrained him. All he could do now was watch as Morrow gave the order for his ship and his allies to open fire on the *Scarlet Wing*. His prized vessel exploded in a cloud of wood and start to slide down into the currents, where it would disappear in the depths. The seat of his power, where he had sailed all over the world and conducted countless raids, was swallowed by the waters it had sailed on for so long.

Morrow looked pleased with the display, despite the fact that the ship had been his home too once. It baffled Ogden that his former first mate could get so much joy from seeing the *Scarlet Wing* fall and disappear from the world above.

Its red sails would never touch the wind again.

"So what now?" Ogden asked. He felt hollow; completely defeated. Part of him was furious that he hadn't seen Morrow's betrayal coming. He knew he was frustrated, but didn't know to what extent. He should have. He should have paid more attention. If he had, all of the crew's under his command, who had trusted him to lead them, might still be alive. The ships they manned might still be afloat. Ogden could still have everything. Instead, he was an admiral without any ships, and with very few men left to command. His life's work had been destroyed.

All that remained was the treasure his shattered fleet had collected, and he was the only one who knew of its location. That gold was all he had left, and he wasn't going to hand it over. Not under any circumstances. Not ever.

"We've crippled your support. England is very interested in the wealth you and I amassed from our pirating. They could put that much wealth to all kinds of uses."

"No, they couldn't," Ogden muttered defiantly. "They won't be touching a single coin of it. Not a single coin. None of you will ever even see it. I can promise you that."

Morrow's expression hardened and he shook his head, leaning in close with his teeth bared. "If you do not cooperate, Walton, we'll have no choice but to have you hanged."

Ogden spat on Morrow's cheek. "I'm one of the most notorious pirates in the world. They are going to hang me either way, whether I cooperate and tell you, or I don't. We both know that, don't we? So there's no point in doing this your way, is there?"

Morrow didn't deny it, and his face was growing red with anger as he wiped the saliva off of his cheek.

"But know this, old friend," Ogden continued venomously. "They can hang me if they like, but when I'm swaying in the air, dangling up there with a broken neck ... when my body is twitching and my face is blue, and breath no longer leaves my body, you will still be no closer to finding what's mine. You never will. Because it's mine. Not yours. It never will be."

Morrow looked like he was holding back an urge to kill Ogden then and there. He even looked like he was contemplating the admiral's words of caution. Even in defeat, Ogden still outmaneuvered him. Morrow was still under his thumb, no matter how much he wanted to increase his station in life. Morrow stepped back and stood over his captive. There was nothing more that could be said between them. They had made their conflicting intentions clear as day. Neither of them would budge or be convinced of anything more.

"Get him out of my sight," Morrow growled.

As Ogden was dragged away, he glared at Morrow and behind that gaze, Morrow saw that Admiral Ogden had gained yet another victory; that even when he lost, he still somehow found a way to win.

8

THE REAL PIRATES

I t had been quite a long boat ride and Purdue was just starting to find his sea legs. He was starting to adjust to the constant swaying of the boat, the smell of the engine on the stern, and even the sight of being in an endless void with no sign of land in any direction.

According to the map, they were nearing the end of their journey. That little island marked by the outlying X was close. As the saying went, it had been clear sailing ever since they got away from Nassau, and would hopefully be just as smooth sailing for the remainder of the voyage.

Unfortunately, as soon as Purdue had that thought, the universe had other plans for him.

Someone was shouting on the boat. Purdue ran across the deck as the rest of the crew all responded and were gathering around as well.

The crew mate hollering was a generally shy and quiet

man named Tevin. In that moment, he was the loudest he had ever been. "The port side! The port side!"

Purdue followed the directions and looked to his left. There were a number of speedboats fast approaching in the distance. Six, at least, cutting through the ocean in a furious dash toward their much slower boat. He pulled up binoculars and looked through them to get a better look at the new arrivals.

Each speedboat had between five and eight men, and they all looked arm with machine guns. AK-47s by the look of it. Guns cheap enough to be easily purchase. They were the weapon of choice among any and all scavengers in the world. Anyone who wanted a taste of power, but couldn't afford anything but the cheapest drop of it.

"Who the hell are they?" Purdue asked, lowering the binoculars and handing them to Aya.

She looked through them and shook her head. "They work for Siad. He considers himself a rival to the Wharf Man, and in some ways, that is what he is. He and his men are pirates. They raid all along these waters."

"Well we're looking for pirate gold ... any chance that we could invoke some ancient pirate tradition and convince them not to start shooting those guns at us. Or maybe even help us?"

"They cannot be reasoned with by words," Aya said. "The only way to negotiate with them is with bullets and blood."

"She is right," Alton said from behind her, leaning against the railing and staring at the oncoming boats. "I suggest you get inside. They are an unpredictable kind of people. I cannot say that there will not be bullets flying through the air any moment now."

Purdue turned to the crew, who all looked nervously out to sea. They didn't want this fight, and he could tell from Aya's explanation that they had known it was a possibility. They hoped that they wouldn't have to get involved with this Siad, but now he was in the way. Whatever blood feud there was between the Wharf Man and Siad would need to be addressed here and now, on these waters, perhaps even on this ship.

What kind of a leader would Purdue be if he hid away and let them deal with it without him? No, he had to stand beside them. After all, he had thrown his hat in with the Wharf Man. As much as he sometimes regretted that alliance, it was an active one, and he was going to respect that. He was going to help however he could.

The speedboats were closing in, cutting across the water. Some broke away from the group, going the other direction. Their plan was obvious to even the most inexperienced of sailors. They were going to encircle the boat. There was no stopping them from ensnaring them with this formation. They couldn't exactly outrun speedboats either.

Purdue stood his ground, which prompted some surprise from the crew. "We fight them off then. I'm not ready to let them come take all of our shit. We've come too far and have far too important of items on board to just let them make off with them. I'm not going to let them touch a damn thing. Are you?"

"No!" Many in the crew yelled back.

The traditional idea of a pirate was mostly a thing of the past. The massive sailboats, the eye patches and peg legs, and the sword duels. It had all been so romanticized over the decades and decades since the golden age of piracy, but pirates themselves still remained. They had just changed, adapted to the times. Traded galleons for speed-boats and flintlocks for automatic machine guns. They no longer went on voyages of pillaging that lasted months or even years. Now they just sped out for day trips and took whatever they could steal from unsuspecting boats.

"You think they know who we are?" Purdue asked.

"I hope not," Aya said. "If they think we are just another boat, then they might just take everything and leave us. If they know we work for the Wharf Man, they will kill us. I am sure of it. And they will make it hurt."

"Perfect," Purdue said uneasily.

"Do not worry yourself," Alton laughed, revealing the pistol in his belt. "My brother and I will protect you from all of the bad men."

Purdue knew that the twins were just as much bad men as the pirates, if not more, but he would take whatever help he could get. In all his travels, he never thought he'd find himself fending off real life pirates.

"We cannot outrun them," Purdue acknowledged.

"So let them come on board," Alton said. "Oniel and I will take it from there."

Oniel silently stared at the enemies who were surrounding them. One of his hands reached into the sleeve of the other, no doubt getting ready to draw a knife whenever he had to. He seemed to prefer blades to firearms. Probably because guns were too loud. Those knives of his were fittingly as quiet as their wielder.

Purdue thought back to the policeman who the twins had disposed of. How his body had gone so limp after Oniel stabbed him in the back. How they had tossed his corpse over the side like it was a bag of garbage. That man was lying on the ocean floor now. Fish and other sea critters were probably picking away at him this very moment. It wasn't a pleasant thought, but that was the kind of action those twins were capable of. Did he want to give them permission to use violence like that again?

No ... not really, but he knew that he really had no say in the matter. If the twins wanted to kill these pirates, they were going to one way or another. Better to direct their inevitable hostilities in a helpful direction than let them get to their killing whenever they felt like it.

He was just glad that they were on his side. "Fine. We'll let them up. Do whatever you have to stop them from taking anything or hurting anyone."

Alton and Oniel both looked a bit surprised with his willingness to let them take control of the situation. Letting them run the show wouldn't be a regular affair though. This was a special case, a situation where he had no choice but to trust their killer instincts to get them all out of this alive.

The pirates were closing in. One pulled up their boat and cut its engine, bobbing gently in the currents beside them. One of the pirates on board stood high and waved his weapon at them. Jermaine looked at Purdue nervously but Purdue nodded, signaling to allow the man on board.

When the pirate climbed up, he had two of his comrades at his side. All three were carrying machine guns and they looked around the boat at the crew. Purdue hung back, looking rather conspicuous. A broke Scottish man standing behind a group of Jamaican criminals.

Alton stepped forward and spoke to the pirates in Somali. He laughed as he spoke, trying to give off an air of ease and cooperation. But while Purdue watched him, he made sure to keep his eye on Oniel who looked tense and ready to start gutting the pirates the moment he had a chance.

Aya translated for Purdue as Alton tried to negotiate with the pirates. Apparently, Alton was trying to surrender and stress that they get this over with as quickly and harmlessly as possible. The lead pirate was snickering now, and Purdue could surmise this part for himself. This was the part when the one with the superior firepower said that the one trying to negotiate was in no position to make any demands. When Aya translated, sure enough, he was right. The pirates under command of the Wharf Man's rival wanted to show their dominance over the situation.

"You do not think I recognize you," the leader suddenly said in unsteady English, examining Alton closely. "I know your face." He pointed at Alton's face and then at Oniel's. "I know that face that you share. That is the face that belongs to the ones who serve the Wharf Man. The twins, yes. Yes that face you both wear is the face of Alton and Oniel, is it not?"

Alton flashed a crooked smile and awkwardly tried to deny it. "I'm sorry but I think you have us mixed up with someone else. Yes we are twins but that is not my name. I am Jermaine. This is my brother, Francis."

The lead pirate laughed. "Is that true, huh? Is it? I am Luka, and I know that I am right. I know that those are not your names, Jermaine. I know because we have been at war with the Wharf Man for some time. Every one of us knows the story of the twins." Luka turned to the two other pirates with him. "The twins have killed many friends of ours, yes?"

The two men nodded and looked ready to raise their machine guns. They were excited by their discovery, like seeing Alton and Oniel was like meeting a pair of celebrities. No, no it there was no reverence in their eyes. There was hunger—they'd just stumbled on a meal that would fill them up for quite some time.

"You have the wrong men," Alton said casually.

"I do?" Luka turned to Oniel. "You. Speak then. Speak."

Oniel stood tall, and looked ready to attack Luka and his men by himself, despite having their guns ready to riddle him with bullets. He wasn't intimidated. If anything, he looked prepared for the challenge, maybe even somewhat excited about it.

"Speak!" Luka barked. "If you can speak then do it now. Prove me wrong."

Oniel remained unfazed by his taunts. He just kept that creepy calmness intact, never batting an eye. Alton, on the other hand, was starting to look nervous.

"Everyone says Oniel does not have a tongue," Luka said. "Open up. Open your mouth. Let us see your tongue and I will admit I was mistaken."

Alton cut in and continued to play dumb but he was far from a professional actor. "There has been some kind of mistake, Luka. My brother and I are fishermen. This is our crew. We are going out into the deep sea and don't want any trouble. We—"

Alton stopped and looked at Luka and his pirates. They weren't buying his story, and he could see that. They had Oniel backed into a corner, waiting for him to speak or prove he had a tongue, neither of which he could do without giving them away. There was no avoiding the truth of their identities, so there was no point keeping up the pretense anymore. Alton flashed that wide Cheshire grin of his and then pulled it back into his face, suddenly looking gravely serious.

"I have heard of you too, Luka," Alton said, all of that jovial friendliness completely gone. "And you have killed many of our men too. Enough that the Wharf Man has put quite a price on your head, hmm?"

"There you are, Alton," Luka said confidently and the men behind him raised their weapons. "I have been wanting to meet you. You and your brother."

"Here we are. You found us."

Alton took a threatening step forward. He towered over Luka and took advantage of their height difference. He had to crane his head down to be eye-to-eye with his enemy. It was clear enough that Luka was the enforcer of that pirate, Siad, just like the twins were the enforcers of the Wharf Man. They were meeting their contemporaries in their rival group, and it looked like a duel was about to break out between the lieutenants of each faction.

"You are out of your waters," Luka said. "The Wharf Man has no control over these waves. This is our ocean, over here. I am sure you must already know that. You have no right to be here."

"No one has complete control over any ocean," Purdue interrupted. "So we have just as much of a right to be here as you, if you ask me."

"I don't remember asking you," Luka said, looking at him with a spiteful leer. "And who is this, hmm?"

"A business partner," Alton said.

"You doing business in our waters. That makes it our business, does it not? So what business are you and this man talking about?"

Alton glanced uneasily at his brother. They were probably considering how well they could kill all three pirates without being gunned down themselves. Before they could start a fight and risk all of their lives, Purdue cut in, opting for negotiation rather than bloodshed.

"They are helping me look for something," Purdue said. The twins looked at him like he was insane for speaking out again, obviously believing that this was none of his business and he should keep out of this feud. Purdue didn't care if they didn't appreciate it. They had already done plenty that he didn't appreciate it. Fair was fair. "A treasure, actually. One that's been missing for centuries."

"Treasure?" Luka started laughing loudly, practically keeling over from the amount of it. "So that is it, hmm? You came here looking for buried treasure. Have you found it?"

"Not yet," Purdue said. "But we are getting very close."

Luka started speaking in his native language again to the two pirates at his side.

Aya once again translated for Purdue, muttering over her shoulder. "They don't seem to believe you. They say that the only treasure in these waters is what they plunder from wandering boats like us. If there was any actual buried treasure, they would have found it by now, they say." She listened intently as Luka spoke once again. "He also thinks that we have brought them the real treasure ... the Wharf Man's men."

Luka turned back to them. "The heads of the twins will make us very rich. Very rich. Treasure, yes. Better than treasure. And we will take whatever you have on this boat too. Payment for crossing our waters."

Purdue didn't particularly like Alton and Oniel but they were his allies and he wasn't willing to just let them be killed by these pirates. Even more, he wouldn't let these scavengers come anywhere close to the relics he had on the boat. They wouldn't take Admiral Ogden's sword or flintlock. He would do whatever he could to prevent that.

Oniel and Alton didn't look too pleased to be threatened either. For the first time, Purdue might have been in exactly the same mindset as the twins. They all understood that they needed to get these pirates off the ship and neutralize the threat as soon as they could. They were getting close to the real prize and they needed to somehow pivot around this last minute obstacle.

Purdue already proved to Alton and Oniel that he didn't support their overly violent methods, but in this case, he might make an exception. Staring down the barrels of those pirates' machine guns helped him make up his mind about it too. These weren't people just trying to apprehend them for committing a crime like those policemen in Nassau. These were people threatening their lives, and threatening everything they had worked for. They would kill Purdue and the whole crew if circumstances called for it, and considering the crew was full of their arch-rival's employees, the circumstances probably called for it.

"You want our heads?" Alton held his arms out in a call for a challenge. "Take them then! That is, if you can."

Before the pirates even had a chance to pull their triggers, the twins threw themselves at the two armed men, knocking them to the floor. Purdue followed their lead—something that surprised even him—and jumped on Luka. The pirate leader threw him off of him almost the moment they hit the deck. The twins seemed to fair better against their opponents, and had gotten a hold of their machine guns. The brothers broke the necks of the pirates with gruesome snaps and Luka ran to the edge of the ship, toward where his allied speedboats were zooming around in the waters. Seeing Alton and Oniel with heavy firepower, he jumped from the boat and went splashing down into the sea.

One of his boats came cutting across the water to pick him up as Purdue and his crew ran to the boats railing to try and pursue. The twins opened fire at the speedboat as Luka climbed up into it and ordered all of the other boats to open fire.

Purdue hit the deck along with everyone else, as bullets bounced all around them, shooting through the air with wild inaccuracy. All of those pirates clearly didn't have the best aim, but with the amount of bullets they were pouring out, it didn't really matter. Alton and Oniel sporadically returned fire. Aya turned to Purdue and the others from across the deck.

"Get us the hell out of here!" Aya yelled. Purdue didn't know what the point of it was. The engine on their boat couldn't exactly outrun the far faster speedboats that were encircling them like a pack of sharks. Aya clearly saw the resilience on Purdue's face and shouted at him once more. Fine! I will do it!"

Aya kept low, hopefully low enough that speedboats around them couldn't see her over the deck, and moved toward the ship's little helm room.

"They're faster than us!" Purdue called over the gunfire as she brushed past him. "We can't get away from them."

"No, not at first!" Aya hollered back. "But we have more gas than them, no? We cannot outrun them, but we can outlast them. We can travel much farther than they can. We have gone off course. Which way to the island?!"

Purdue was hesitant. Part of him didn't want to risk luring those pirates anywhere close to Admiral Ogden's treasure. He didn't want to have to deal with them along with the uncertainty he already had about some members of his own crew.

If only these pirates weren't such ferocious enemies with the Wharf Man, maybe this wouldn't have blown into something so violent, where he and anyone on his crew could be killed at any moment. All it took was one stray bullet. Once again, the Wharf Man's presence and influence was negatively effecting this whole voyage. If it wasn't the deranged twins killing innocent people, then it was the enemies of the Jamaican crime boss trying to get retribution for grievances that had nothing to do with Purdue.

"Which way?!" Aya had control of the wheel now and her other hand on the ship's throttle. The small windows of the helm room shattered and she ducked to avoid the bullets spraying all over the place.

Purdue had to finish weighing his options, and fast. If they waited any longer, sitting out in the open sea at the mercy of these speedboats, the pirates would grow bold enough to jump back onto the ship and retake control of the whole situation.

"That way!" Purdue pointed west. "We need to head in that direction!"

That sealed it. He hoped she was right that those little speedboats didn't have much gas to spare. They weren't meant for long trips, so hopefully they would eventually have to fall behind. It all depended on Purdue's crew living that long. They had to keep avoiding the bullets that were raining down on them.

Aya nodded and pushed the throttle forward. Their ship's propellers kicked in and they started moving forward as Aya steered them in the right direction. There was shouting from around them, the pirates calling to one another to adapt to their prey trying to escape.

Both of the twins' AK-47's were out of ammunition, so they threw the weapons overboard. Everyone still kept their heads down as the speedboats turned on their own engines and began chasing after them. They caught up as quickly as expected, and Purdue doubted that they would be able to hold out long enough for the speedboats to run out of fuel and completely fall behind. And if they reached their destination before that happened, then they will have brought their enemies to what they most needed to protect. They would all be killed when they reached the shore, and the pirates might even find the gold that had been hidden by another group of pirates centuries beforehand.

They moved through the water for hours, keeping low. By that point, the gun fire coming from the pursuing speedboats had ceased. They couldn't be sure if the pirate gang had run out of ammunition or if they were just through wasting it until they could actually hit their targets. Just to be safe, everyone on board Purdue's ship kept themselves low. They couldn't afford to lose anyone. Alton and Oniel crawled about and both looked humiliated by having to slink around like cowards, but they could stow their pride if it meant staying alive.

Purdue kept hunched down near the helm, helping make sure they were keeping on the right path to the island. Every so often, he would look back and the speedboats would still be following. Whatever bad blood there was between these Somalian pirates and the Wharf Man, it was bad enough that they weren't giving up in their pursuit easily. However, he did notice they were starting to fall behind a bit, maybe slowing down to conserve their fuel. Hopefully that meant they were getting low, and they didn't have any more emergency reserves.

Maybe this plan, this battle of stamina between two kinds of sea vessels, would work after all.

"There's something up ahead!" one of the crew shouted from toward the bow of the boat. "Something in the distance!"

Purdue peaked up with Aya at the horizon ahead of them, being sure to keep their heads low as they looked. There was something far away—land. It was an island, alright, and not a large one. It was probably the same size of land mass as what was shown on the map, as the shape that was crossed out with that telltale X.

Most likely their destination, and the resting place of Admiral Ogden's treasure.

Just as Purdue feared, Luka and the rest of Siad's pirates were still following. They either needed to pull away from the island and go in a different direction, somehow beat the pirates right there and then, or in the worst case scenario, try and face them on the island. Whatever they chose, they had to choose it soon.

"Should we keep going forward?" Aya asked, cautiously reaching up toward the ship's controls. "Or do we veer away."

If they kept trying to take them on in the water, they wouldn't be able to fight them off. They were already outgunned and outnumbered. They would be overrun if they kept this up. On land, they at least had a chance to fight on even grounds rather than their enemy being able to outmaneuver them. They would still be outnumbered and outgunned but they could fight back on land rather than sit there hoping not to get shot like they had been doing on the boat.

"Stay on course," Purdue said. "Let's get to that damn island already."

"Bring them to the treasure?" Alton called over from where he was crouched down. "Have you lost your mind?"

"No," Purdue said. "We won't let them get that far. I'm counting on you and Oniel to make sure of that."

The twins looked at one another and both seemed to be filled with a newfound excitement. They loved a good fight, and best of all, they were good at it. Hopefully, they would be the deciding factor in their victory. They may not have the numbers, but Purdue felt like they had the ingenuity to overcome the disadvantages they had.

Purdue looked at the island drawing closer and then leaned back and peeked at the boats that were still on their trail. They seemed to be speeding up, no doubt concluding that their prey were heading to land. "Once we get close, we all need to get off the ship as quickly as possible to ambush those bastards. If we can't surprise them, then they won't have any trouble just gunning us down."

The island was fast approaching and Aya slowed the ship down with a pull of the throttle as they approached the shore. There was a rocking beneath him of the keel touching shallower waters and as it slowed, the whole crew hurried across the deck, climbing down and splashing down onto the rocky beach of the island.

Purdue was the last off of the boat, and ran across the deck. He turned to check on the pirates' location and was met by flashing gunfire rocketing toward them in the water. He ducked for cover and then jumped off the boat.

His feet touched down on the shoreline, and a feeling swept over him.

This was it. The place that could make him rich again.

Admiral Ogden missed the ocean. He missed the vast openness that he was able to explore while sailing the seas. He missed the ability to potentially go anywhere in the world, to explore faraway places to his heart's content. He missed his freedom.

Now, all he had was a cramped and dark dungeon cell, awaiting his sentence. He knew what his punishment would be. He was a pirate after all, and there was only one real way the crown dealt with pirates. They had to be made examples of. Their rebelliousness and lawlessness had to be purged from the world. A pirate wouldn't just rot away in a dungeon forever. No. A pirate would become a hanging carcass for the whole world to see, a warning to the people to never consider becoming one. That was Ogden's fate, and he had come to accept it. Now he just wanted to get it over with.

He sat on the cold floor of his cell, picking at the stone wall because there was nothing better to do. He had to find some way to pass the time. Who knew how long it would be until they could finally just get on with it?

The door down the corridor opened and he heard some guards stationed there speaking to someone. Ogden waited patiently as footsteps came down the hall, out of sight. It could have just been another arrest and someone was going to be thrown into another cage, but it kept coming closer. He was certain his was the last cell in the chamber so they couldn't be going past him. When the door to his holding cell opened, two guards were flanking a young woman who Ogden recognized.

The lady from the tavern during that hurricane —Victoria.

"Are you sound about this, miss?"

"I am," she said to the guards. "Thank you."

The two guards looked hesitant to leave and one of them turned his attention to his prisoner. "Don't try anything, admiral. We will be just outside."

"Thank you," Victoria said again and the guards respectfully stepped out, closing the door and leaving Ogden alone with the woman he barely knew. She regarded him just like she had at the dinner table, with keen interest like she was observing some kind of wild animal that she didn't fully understand. From what he remembered, she came from wealth and had been pampered her whole life. Piracy itself confounded her. She couldn't grasp why anyone would be commit crimes to try and improve their lives.

Ogden didn't stand to greet her. He barely had enough strength to, but even if he did, he would have remained sitting lazily against the wall. At this point in the fleeting time he had left, manners were some of the least of his concerns.

"I remember you," Ogden said from the floor.

"And I you," she replied with a curtsy. "It is nice to see you again, Admiral Ogden."

"Is it?" Ogden snorted. "Must be great to see me awaiting the gallows. Not that it isn't a pleasure to see you again, but what exactly is it you're doing here? Came to see the show?"

"I had to see you again before..."

"Before my neck breaks and the stench of my rotting corpse starts spreading all over the streets of London?"

She looked hurt by his insinuation that she would take any pleasure in his death, but frankly, he was baffled that she was even there. There didn't seem to be any sensible reason why she would want to visit him. They had one mildly interesting conversation once and suddenly she was here, to have one more before he died?

A thought occurred to him and it seemed like the only possibility that made sense. Morrow had been there that night, drinking in the tavern with the rest of the crew. He had seen Ogden speaking with Victoria for quite some time, maybe even surmised that the conversation had been more than just a passing distraction.

"Did Morrow send you here to convince me to give up the treasure's location?"

She raised a brow and looked completely confused by the question. "No, who is Morrow?"

"Jacob Morrow. Former first mate of the *Scarlet Wing*. Current captain of the *Iron Horn*. A proud privateer who sold his soul to the king. A disloyal weasel who turned against all of his brothers and is the sole reason that I am stuck in this dry cave instead of being out in the open sea. That is Morrow. Did he ask you to come speak with me?"

"No," Victoria insisted. "No, I'm afraid I've never even met the man."

She looked sincere enough, but Ogden was still reeling from the hard lesson he learned about lies and trust. Her denials could just be her trying to preserve the innocent facade while she tried to coax the location of the treasure out of him. If that was the case, it wasn't going to work on him. Morrow would have to try harder if he really wanted to find it.

"Then what do you want?" He asked, more aggressively than he intended.

Victoria took a step away, back toward the door. She looked ready to leave, probably regretting that she had ever come at all but she took a breath and didn't retreat any further.

"You always fascinated me," she said.

Ogden remembered that much. Victoria had loved the tall tales people talked about; she believed them even. The stories that he coated his sails in blood or commanded an absurd amount of men in his pirate navy. She had painted a particularly grandiose picture of him in her imagination and that night at the tavern, she discovered that pirates were people. They were human beings who were desperate, looking for purpose, and often times just cruel, but people nonetheless. He left that conversation hoping that she could now see reality a little more clearly.

"And even now, you fascinate me still," she took a surprising step forward. "I had to beg my father to use his influence to allow me to come visit you. He never understood my interest in pirates. He never saw what I do. He never stopped to wonder about that fact that all of you, you pirates, always know that your actions could bring you to this place. You know that you can end right up here, having to face a horrible death in front of an audience ... but you still break the laws anyway."

"Why let something as trivial as law and order stop you from living your best life, hmm?" Ogden said rather nonchalantly.

"I just want to understand," Victoria said.

"You never will," Ogden said bluntly. "Look at you. You have a good life, a safe life. You have never been at the bottom. Down there, you are treated like you are nothing.

You've never had your superiors act like your life is disposable. I, like all of the late members of my destroyed fleet, understood that and that is why they sailed with me. We all wanted something more, and we wanted to get it without anyone being able to tell us that we couldn't. To live without restraint is true freedom. That is what the sea brings. That is how we have lived."

Victoria was silent, now staring at the gray floor of the cell. "Was it worth it?"

Ogden laughed and unsteadily got to his feet. He limped over to her and gently touched her chin, tilting her head upward so her gaze was brought from the floor to his eyes. He wanted her to see his own eyes and just how serious he was about his answer. "Absolutely. I got everything I wanted."

"You did?"

"I thought I wanted more. I tried to get more. But in the end ... that's what got me caught. That's why I am in this damn cell. I had acquired more wealth than I knew what to do with, and I somehow still wanted more. Enough wasn't enough for me. If I had been more content with what I already had..." He stopped, and felt foolish to be regretting anything. Regret wouldn't do him any good at all. He changed the course of his thoughts. "The point is, I hate that I was caught and I hate how it happened, but I don't for a moment hate the lifestyle I chose. If you ask me, in this age, it is the only way to live truly free."

"I'm sorry," Victoria said after a long moment. "I'm sorry

that you're going to die."

"Don't be," Ogden said with a shrug. "It is what it is. Death was bound to happen someday. And perhaps you will hear even better tales about my death. Maybe they will say that I didn't die on the hangman's noose, not until they had to tear my head from my body completely. Or perhaps they will say that the man who will be executed wasn't me at all, a clever decoy while the real Admiral Ogden is still out there, ravaging the high seas. Who knows? Maybe I am a decoy."

"You're not," she laughed.

"Are you sure? All you have to go on is the word of a pirate," Ogden snickered. "I could have lied to you in that tavern. This all could have been an elaborate ruse."

"Perhaps," Victoria conceded, still laughing. An uneasy tension returned as the impending execution loomed over them. "If the real Admiral Ogden is out there, then I hope to meet him at some point ... but if, as I suspect, you are indeed the true admiral, then I am glad to have met you. I'm glad to have had these conversations, no matter how brief they were. They might all say you're a monster, but please know that I don't think that anymore."

"I appreciate that," Ogden said. "At least there will be one person who doesn't spit on my swaying body. Are you ... are you going to watch the execution? Or are proper young women not allowed to view such a show?"

"I don't want to see it," Victoria said. "But I will. I will be there for you in those last moments."

"Thank you," Ogden said. "It was a pleasure speaking with you, Victoria."

"It was a pleasure to speak to you as well, Admiral Ogden."

She turned to leave and he called after her. "You never did ask about the gold."

Victoria swung back around and looked at him again with confusion. "Was I supposed to?"

"I'm sure it's what most people will be interested in after my death. I supposed that you would be just as curious about it."

"Your treasure does not interest me nearly as much as the man who collected it." She smiled at him and he unconsciously returned his own smile. She really hadn't been sent by Morrow. Her visit wasn't a trick; she genuinely cared. She lingered for a moment longer, her lips still stretched into the pleasant smile he first saw in that tavern. "Goodbye."

After she left, Ogden found himself alone in complete isolation in the dungeon again. He still longed for the sea and all of its luxuries and thrills. He still dreaded his oncoming execution, of course, but something was different now. He felt a comfort that he hadn't felt since losing his crew. As lonely as he felt in the dungeon, at least he knew he wouldn't be alone when he died. Someone would mourn him. That was a comfort, if only a little one.

9

THE DESTINATION

They made it—the small island from the map. The one bearing the only true X on those charts. The supposed resting place of one of the largest hoards of treasure ever collected in one place. Although, that depended on if Purdue was right and he had been able to actually decipher the map, and not just notice a mistake that Admiral Ogden made. They would find out soon enough, but he couldn't shake the feeling that this was the right place to be if he needed to improve his finances.

First, they had murderous modern-day pirates to deal with.

"To the trees!" Aya yelled out and everyone followed her toward the line of tree trunks leading to a jungle.

They were sprinting as fast as they could, no one daring to see the progress Luka and his pirates were making for their landing. Once under the cover of the trees, everyone took positions behind the trunks, or climbed up into the branches to see where their enemy was. The pirates had already made their landing, their speedboats sliding right onto the rocky shore, and they were hopping out of their vehicles, moving toward the jungle with their machine guns raised. It reminded Purdue of some sort of criminal D-Day, and unfortunately for him and his crew, they weren't able to bombard the invaders on the shore with gunfire and missiles. Instead, they were going to have to rely on their wits and the crucial element of surprise to seize victory.

The most important thing to Purdue was staying alive. He didn't come all this way and find this godforsaken island just to die; he couldn't let that happen, not when he was so close. That treasure could be mere steps away. They had to see this through. The appearance of these pirates couldn't derail everything. It just needed to be another obstacle that he could overcome, just like the museum and the unpredictability of the twins. They needed to beat these pirates before Luka and his boys had a chance to kill them first.

The pirates were nearly upon them. Purdue was pinned against the backside of a thick trunk, out of view from the oncoming enemies. Everyone else had just as effective hiding spots and Purdue glanced at Alton who was crouching behind a nearby brush. They locked eyes and Purdue nodded to him. Without words, they both knew they were thinking the same thought—the second these pirates crossed the tree line ... that would be the time to jump them. In the close quarters of the jungle, and with all of the trees in the way, their AK-47's might lose some of their usefulness ... at least, that was Purdue's hope.

Many had armed themselves with whatever they could find. Some picked up rocks from the ground and cupped them in their hands. Others like Purdue found thick branches to use as weapons. Oniel was the only one with an actual weapon, having held onto the knife that he stabbed that Nassau police officer with. While Purdue still objected to that killing, he wouldn't be so against Oniel putting his killer instincts to work in the same of defending all of them.

The footsteps were getting closer and out of the corner of his eye, a barrel of a machine gun moved right past Purdue's face from the other side of the tree. A man followed the weapon and then a man came from Purdue's other side, and then more entered the jungle.

If they jumped out too soon, the remaining pirates would remain at the tree line and just riddle the jungle with bullets. They needed to let enough of them inside to make for an effective ambush. Luckily, the pirates didn't seem to expect that Purdue and his crew were waiting and instead moved straight through without a second look. They thought Purdue and the others were fleeing through the jungle, not waiting for them.

This was their chance—and Purdue took it.

After letting a fourth man pass, Purdue launched the fight into motion by swinging his branch into the next man's face. The moment that wood made contact with the man's dark face and knocked him over, chaos exploded throughout the trees. All of Purdue's allies pounced on the pirates who didn't even have a moment to react to the sudden attack. It turned into a catastrophic brawl. A few gunshots rang out but most of the pirates didn't even have a chance to fire their machine guns. They were being swarmed and beaten down.

Luka retreated backward, fear in his eyes, and he yelled out orders to his men. They couldn't hear him. They were too busy getting their teeth kicked in by Purdue and his crew. Unlike his men, Luka wasn't armed with an AK-47, and Purdue was especially thankful for that. If Luka wanted to survive, he'd either have to run, fight them hand to hand, or try and get one of his men's guns, putting himself at risk. To their luck, he chose the last option and sprinted into the fray, hoping to pick up one of the dropped weapons. He managed to get a hold of one of his fallen brothers' guns and turned it in the direction of the fight. He looked ready to gun down everyone, including his own men, but Purdue was already upon him.

Wielding his tree branch like a baseball bat, Purdue swung hard and made contact with the AK-47, knocking it out of Luka's hands before he had a chance to unleash his ammunition. Luka tried to get away from him, tripping over some roots as Purdue continued on him. Seeing how callously he was about to get rid of his own men, Purdue didn't want to show someone like that any mercy. He wanted to knock him around and teach him a lesson about consequences. He chose to be a pirate. He chose to threaten and attack people, all so he could pick at scraps left behind by his victims. Purdue would make sure that Luka was going to answer for all of his heinous crimes.

He hit him hard again with the branch, knocking the wind out of him, and Luka rolled away desperately.

The fight around them was slowing down, with Purdue's crew clenching a decisive victory. Their ambush had gone perfectly and the pirates were all incapacitated. Some were dead while others were just beaten into submission. Oniel collected the magazines from all of their machine guns and then threw them in various directions through the jungle. His message was clear enough; that there was no need for that kind of firepower on this island. Part of Purdue later wondered if Oniel was just trying to make sure that him and his knife remained the deadliest weapons on that slice of land.

Luka was on his knees with a scrape over his eye and a bruised lip. He was breathing heavily and looking around at his men with disappointment. Purdue held the branch over his head, ready to bring it down on the pirate leader. At the very least, he could knock him out. The blow might even bash his skull in. Purdue didn't want to kill Luka. He didn't want to kill anyone, but in this situation, there might not have been much of a choice at all. This man's only desire was to cause violence.

"Go on," Alton said. "Believe me, they more than deserve it. Siad's pirates have been a scourge on the water for years. No one will miss them. Not even their own mothers."

Luka glared up a him. He smacked his hands on his upper torso in a gesture of challenge. "You heard him! It is all true! Kill me then unless you don't got the stomach for it!"

Purdue wondered that himself, and his stomach seemed to churn as he did. He didn't feel right bludgeoning an unarmed man to death as part of some execution. That wasn't him. He turned to Alton who kept urging him to just do it. In that moment, he realized that the man he was about to beat to death wasn't much different than some of his own crew, the twins in particular. If he could work with them, converse with them, and even respect them sometimes, despite how vicious of people they were and the killings they committed, then he would be a hypocrite to kill Luka and spare them. No, he wouldn't kill Luka. He was just a threat that needed to be neutralized while they found the gold.

Purdue stepped away from the defeated pirate beneath him. Alton's mouth was hanging open and he looked at Purdue like he was insane, before taking a step toward Luka himself, but Purdue grabbed his arm. "No. Tie him and any of his remaining men up. I think there's been enough violence today, don't you?"

"Some days require more blood than others," Alton hissed. Purdue couldn't entirely blame him. It sounded like a long, violent history between the two groups. Alton probably had good reason to want to smash Luka's brains in, but as long as Purdue was there, they had other things to focus on.

"Not today," Purdue said. "Put aside all of that petty shit for now, aye? We need to find the treasure. That's what we need to be thinking about right now. Not some old blood war. The treasure takes priority right now."

Alton glared down at Luka and didn't look at all pleased with this decision. In fact, he looked ready to rip Luka's limbs off. Finally, he conceded and seemed to relax. "Fine. He will live."

Purdue removed his hand from restraining Alton and breathed a sigh of relief. However, the second he let go Alton threw a punch that struck Luka hard in the jaw and knocked him onto his back.

"Hey!" Purdue yelled, grabbing hold of him again. He should have known better than expecting either of the twins to show any sort of restraint. They certainly hadn't back in Nassau with that policeman.

Alton turned back to Purdue and that fake smile of his returned to his face. He pointed at Luka groaning on the ground. "What? I told you, he still lives."

"You still didn't need to do that," Purdue said, scratching his head.

Alton glanced back down at Luka and spat on the ground. "Yes I did."

The crew got to tying up the pirates to some of the trees in the jungle, making sure each of them was well restrained so they didn't risk coming back after them. They could figure out what to do with them after they found the treasure.

With their enemies out of the way, the crew moved through the jungle, looking for anything out of the ordinary. The jungle was lush but not very big so it didn't take them long to cover a lot of ground. The island itself was so small, it didn't leave many possible hiding places for Admiral Ogden to have chosen. As they searched, Purdue started to feel a little worried. Perhaps the island was too remote, and tiny to be the place where the enormous stockpile of gold to be hidden. Then again, being so small and far away from society, might make it the perfect island for such a task.

"This is the place?" Alton asked.

"It is," Purdue replied. "This is the place shown on the map."

"It does not look like much," Alton said, looking around.

"What were you expecting, aye? Skull Island?"

"That would have been better than this," Alton muttered. "There is nothing here. This has all been a waste. When the Wharf Man finds out—"

Alton tripped over a slab of rock and fell hard onto his stomach. Purdue almost let out a laugh, glad to see that cocky bastard finally make a mistake. Still, he held out a hand to help him up just out of respect. Alton, looking flustered with embarrassment, smacked Purdue's hand away and stood up by himself, looking down at what had knocked him over. He looked ready to murder the earth itself for taking a shot at him.

There were two large slabs of stone crossing over one another on the ground. They stood out from the ground around them, which was almost barren of any sort of plants or other rocks. The whole section of the island looked a little strange, like it hadn't been created in the same way as everything else on the island, like it didn't really belong there. The large slabs were embedded in the ground and looked to have been there for quite some time, but not quite as long as all of the old roots and trees of the island.

The strangest thing was that those two rocks on the ground—they sort of made an X if you were looking at them from above. The whole crew huddled around the intertwined rocks and everyone seemed to be putting together the same thought. Given the Xs that Admiral Ogden used to designate the treasure's location on his flintlock and map, it wasn't an improbable thought that he would use the X as a tool when it came to hiding his treasure as well.

"X marks the spot, aye?" Purdue said aloud, voicing everyone's shared thought.

"It better," Alton said, still looking flustered but now also looking frustrated. "You seemed certain in your ability to read the map before. So is this it or not?"

"I wasn't certain," Purdue said defensively, remembering

a very different conversation that they had back when he was trying to figure out the map. "I said that this island seemed like it was the right place as long as my theory was correct. It was just at that. A theory. I still might be wrong."

Alton looked uncharacteristically displeased. All of that jovial fake friendliness he put on was nowhere to be found. He looked impatient, like he wasn't going to even bother with his usual boasting. He clearly wanted this to be the right place, and part of Purdue wondered what Alton would do if it wasn't.

They grabbed the shovels and started digging around the X. Strangely, the ground around the rocks didn't feel very solid. After a couple of minutes, Purdue struck the ground with the spade and suddenly felt his body quake. The earth underneath him gave way and he went sliding through the ground, tumbling down into the mud and dirt underneath the island.

His body finally stopped when he landed hard on his stomach. He took a minute to try and get up and when he did, his hand touching something different than the earth. He touched something smooth and small ,and when he took hold of it, he held it close to his eyes. It was a coin. A very old piece of gold.

He pulled himself up, still fixated on the coin in his hand and swearing under his breath. He struggled to look away from the coin but when he did, he found himself in a large cave. He'd fallen through something of a tunnel that led to a far bigger space. It was like he had ridden a slide to some secret underground chamber.

"Purdue!"

There were shouts behind him, through the narrow tunnel that had carried him there. It was the crew, calling down from the sunlight above.

"Are you alive?!" Aya's voice shouted down.

"I'm alright!" Purdue shouted back up before focusing on what was in front of him and then back to the piece of gold. "More than alright, actually!"

He took a few steps into the new place he found and his whole body was filling with excitement, because the cavern he was looking in wasn't empty. The coin in his hand was not the only coin inside of the cave either. It was one of probably millions of others piled about.

Purdue was staring at the treasure of Admiral Ogden.

The morning of Admiral Walton Ogden's execution, the streets of London were bristling with anticipation. Everyone was looking forward to catching a glimpse of the famed pirate, and better yet, they got to see his end when justice finally caught up with him.

Admiral Ogden stood tall on the execution platform, undeterred by the noose around his neck and by the crowd of spectators who were hungrily awaiting his death. They shouted obscenities at him. Some threw rocks and fruits his way with varying levels of accuracy. Others clapped and cheered. He wasn't afraid of any of the spectacle. He didn't mind if his death got an applause since he couldn't entirely blame them. His reputation and occupation hadn't painted him in the best light to the public. To most people, he was the scourge of the seven seas. He was a rebel who plagued all manner of law and authority. He was a demon waving a black flag, killing anyone in his path. A monster whose only desire was destruction.

The stories weren't entirely wrong but they were also far from the truth. He was absolutely rebellious and could even be ruthless when the circumstances called for it, but he was not some evil sea demon making sacrifices to the devil. Walton Ogden was just a man who wanted fame and fortune. He may have wanted it too much, but who didn't want those things in life? And how few actually achieved either? He had attained both. While his life turned out shorter than expected, he took solace that he had gotten what he wanted in life.

Morrow stood on a nearby balcony watching the macabre presentation unfold. He made sure to meet eyes with Ogden, offering a wink that oozed with pomposity. This must have been the proudest moment of his miserable life. It didn't matter to Ogden because he knew full well that Morrow wouldn't win in the end. Ogden had made sure he would never, ever find the treasure.

An official read off a list of Ogden's numerous crimes and

Ogden let each one pass through his thoughts, retracing them in his memory. His whole life as a pirate was unfolded before him, and forced in front of his eyes. As he thought about each event listed to him, he realized—to his own surprise—that he regretted none of them. They were crimes, yes, but each was a stepping stone on his path to success. Everything he had worked for was still there, and still safe, whether he was breathing or not.

As his crimes were recounted, he scanned the crowd of faces, past Morrow and all of the peasants throwing rocks at him, past the guards in their red uniforms, and past the children watching through the gaps of their fingers.

Finally, he found her. Victoria stood near the back of the crowd with a man Ogden recognized as her father. She had come after all and when their eyes met, she offered a warm smile. Even as the cold touch of death was starting to touch him, he could feel her smile. He wasn't going to die surrounded entirely by people that wanted him dead. There was at least one who wouldn't be celebrating his demise.

"If you have any final words, now is the time to share them. Perhaps God will hear your pleas for forgiveness."

Admiral Ogden laughed. "I don't much care for his forgiveness, and I never plead for anything from anyone ... not even that bastard in heaven above. Everything I have done has been through sheer force of will alone. My will. Not God's. Mine. My own fortitude and determination to see my dream made reality. That is something most of you standing here, ready to see me hang, will never understand. You are content watching better people find success or find failure, while you stand there comfortable with your petty jealousies and insignificant problems. I see you for exactly what you are."

Ogden's gaze scanned the crowd and fixed on Morrow.

"All of you. You are all just vultures, waiting for a chance to pick apart anything vulnerable. Anything that is already down and wounded. You're all cowards and you're all pathetic."

There were boos and shouts from the crowd of spectators. Some more stones were thrown in his direction. He let them bounce off like they weren't a bother at all. The audience was turning into an angry mob, ready to storm the gallows and break his neck themselves.

Ogden raised his voice, to be heard over their heckling. "I possess more gold than any of you will ever see in your lives. More gold than any of you can even begin to fathom. However much your imagination concocts, it's more. Believe me. You vultures won't be able to pick me apart for all I'm worth. You will never find what I leave behind."

Ogden half-expected the hangman to grow bored with his speech and pull the lever, but he didn't. He even seemed enthralled by the pirate's speech, hanging onto every word.

"Someone may find it one day, but it won't be any of you. No. It would take a special kind of person to find my treasure. Only someone worthy will be able to inherit my legacy. As for the rest of you sorry lot ... I hope you enjoy failing to find it."

Up on the balcony, Morrow was shaking his head, obviously not impressed by Ogden's defiant words. The spectators all looked entirely flabbergasted by his speech, but behind all of them, there was Victoria who was beaming with pride. Hopefully now, at the end, she fully understood where he was coming from. If that's all he had accomplished, then at least he had done that.

Admiral Ogden turned to the hangman. "Come on then. Get on with it."

The hangman came out of his stupor and looked to the officials for approval. He got a nod in response and then gave the lever a good pull.

The platform beneath Ogden's feet fell away and he dropped down. He was caught by the noose around his throat, but his neck didn't break. Instead, he swayed in the air, his body twitching as he slowly choked to death in front of the audience of bloodthirsty, law-abiding citizens. They got the show they wanted. They got to see the infamous pirate admiral be hanged for all of his monstrous crimes. However, many left the gruesome display feeling unsettled. Admiral Ogden's final words, his taunts about his treasure, had cut deep as any sword.

No one had been punctured by the pirates speech more deeply than Jacob Morrow. He stayed at the execution ground for hours after the rest of the audience had gone about their day. He stared up at Ogden's swaying body and among his disdain, jealousy, and resentment, there was a strange tingle of guilt; a feeling that he should be hanging up there with his old friend. But that feeling washed away after a few fleeting moments, and his bitterness returned.

Morrow had beaten Admiral Ogden yet the pirate acted like the victor, even going so far as to make a triumphant speech as he stood on the execution platform, on death's door itself. Morrow couldn't accept losing to a dead man, to someone that he thought he had defeated. He would prove Ogden wrong and he would find that treasure.

Jacob Morrow tried—for decades—to find the resting place of his old captain's gold. He scoured the known world but found nothing. He eventually died at an old age, spiteful of how he had wasted so much of his life in search of something he could never find. There was nothing to show for all of his efforts in the end. He even felt regretful of the betrayal that started his spiral.

Many tried looking for the treasure, inspired by Admiral Ogden's famous proclamation and challenge he had made with a noose around his neck. However, all who tried failed miserably. None of them proved to be worthy of finding the treasure. They weren't the special person that Ogden hoped would inherit his vast wealth.

That person had yet to come.

10

SHINING MOUNTAINS

The entire cavern was filled with enormous piles of gold and other valuables. Jewelry, silverware, and all kind of trinkets were dispersed throughout the golden hills. They all stood before gleaming mountains of old currency and souvenirs from pillaged vessels. The entire collection of Admiral Walton Ogden's fleet. The trophies of their efforts to raid the high seas.

Purdue knew what it was like to have such a vast collection—and he knew how it felt to lose it.

Admiral Ogden was lucky to not live to see his prizes stolen from him, and all of his efforts gone to waste. He wasn't going to have to experience that loss like Purdue had. Even though they were being taken, Ogden's cherished possessions weren't going to go to waste. Despite being long dead, Admiral Ogden and his treasure would help Purdue bring down one of the greatest dangers to the world.

As the crew moved through the cavern, their feet crunched over large coins and accidentally kicked around other trinkets. Everyone looked around in awe of the treasure hoard around them, overwhelmed by the possibility that these riches could bring. Their lives could be changed for the better.

Even the usually dour Oniel had a small smile on his face. He didn't look quite right with it. The smile didn't fit the silent sourpuss that Purdue had come to know and loath.

Alton cupped a pile of gold coins in his hands and tossed them up into the air, laughing as they rained down on him. There were howls of celebration from the whole crew. People hugged and cheered, practically dancing around the stockpile of riches.

Purdue himself was surprised by the sheer amount of treasure that was in front of him. He expected a lot, but this ... this was beyond anything his imagination could have concocted. The amount of time and work it must have taken for Ogden's fleet to acquire so much ... it was mind-boggling.

Worry crept into his thoughts, and he was about to speak that newfound fear aloud, when Aya beat him to it. She apparently shared his concern.

"We're not going to be able to get all of this onto the ship," Aya said.

"Aye," Purdue said with a nod. "The Wharf Man should have loaned me a bigger one."

Aya took a breath, letting herself relax and just be happy with the outcome of their search. She turned to Purdue with a wide smirk. "You really did it."

"Of course I did," Purdue said, also trying to stow away his worries for now and just enjoy the victory. They could deal with the semantics later. "I'm insulted that there was ever any doubt."

Alton had heard their worries though and strolled over with utmost confidence, like he already had everything all figured out. He held up his large radio and waved it at them. "I will contact the Wharf Man and have him send more ships to take all of this back. Believe me, he will send a whole fleet to ferry his prize."

Purdue almost choked on his own spit. "His prize? Partially, aye. Most of this is going where I want it to. He can do what he pleases with the thirty percent he was promised."

Alton looked flustered, like he had just been caught in a lie. Maybe he had. He had firmly planted his foot in his mouth and clearly knew that everyone had heard him do it. His face slipped back into that arrogant smile, but it seemed more crooked than usual. "Of course. My English is not great. Let me try to say it again."

Funny, because Purdue had been impressed with Alton's mastery of English throughout the whole voyage. He didn't seem to ever have had a slip up like that before.

Purdue felt his blood starting to boil and suddenly the world around him seemed to be shining a light on Alton; an intense, focused beam of light like he was sitting in the middle of an interrogation. Everything else fell away and Purdue could only focus on the expression on Alton's face.

Alton looked back at Purdue, and then his usually perfect smile grinded together uncomfortably. He looked guilty. No, he was guilty.

The more outgoing of the twins snickered awkwardly. He was like a boy being caught stealing from the cookie jar. He knew now that there was no excuse that could get him out of the mistake he'd made. The jig was up, and whatever game he was playing was over.

"Come on, Purdue," Alton said, straightening his posture. "You had to know that this was how it was going to go. The Wharf Man does not settle for portions! He is the one that decides who gets what, and you will take whatever scraps he gives you."

"That wasn't the arrangement."

"There was no arrangement," Alton said sternly. "There was only talking. Talking, talking, talking. That's all it was. What is that expression? That action is far louder than any words that are spoken? The Wharf Man does not negotiate. He takes what he wants. And he wants this treasure that you so kindly told him about."

Purdue shook his head. He should have known better

than to trust the Wharf Man and his goons. He had known better, he'd just second guessed himself. In this desperate time, he had to accept friendship where he could find it, even if it left him vulnerable to this exact kind of betrayal.

"Oh, I see ... so your boss is a liar and a con man. We made a deal. Me and him. And whether he likes it or not, that means something. He is going to follow through on his end."

"No," Alton said. "You will take whatever he decides you earned. Even if it is nothing. You will be thankful, because none of it is yours. It is only by his mercy, that you receive anything."

Purdue clenched his fist and took a step forward. While Alton was taller than him, he had to stand up to him. He wouldn't let them stab him in the back. They could try, but he would make sure that he came out on top. He wouldn't let someone else take anything from him. He'd let that happen long enough. It was time to protect what was rightfully his.

"We both know that that's shit, and it's not going to happen."

Beside Alton, Oniel drew a knife in one precise motion, staring at Purdue. He'd probably been itching to kill him this whole voyage. And now he might get the chance.

Alton didn't acknowledge the blade in his brother's hand. He just laughed at Purdue. "We needed you for your map. We needed you because you are good at finding things. We needed something found, and you found it. Your job is done, hmm? Understand me?"

Purdue was outnumbered and he had seen how quickly Oniel could plunge that little blade into someone. He knew how deadly his newfound enemies were. He wouldn't stand a chance in a fight against them, but he wouldn't relent.

"Well, if there's no deal, then I don't owe the Wharf Man any of it either then."

Oniel took a step forward, looking ready to slip that knife into Purdue's eye sockets.

To Purdue's surprise, the rest of the crew moved in front of him. They formed a protective barrier of bodies between Purdue and the twins. Nearly a dozen people were in between Purdue and Oniel's knife.

"What is this?" Alton barely managed to hold in another giggle.

"You are not going to touch him," Aya said firmly from the front of the pack.

"We're not?" Alton looked at his brother, who looked ready to tear apart the wall of bodies that were in his way. Neither of them looked overly concerned by the obstacle. If anything, they looked excited by the challenge.

"Purdue is going to let us have much more gold than the Wharf Man would. We'd be lucky if we got anything from him. Purdue will be far better for us."

Alton put a hand on his forehead in agitation but kept laughing. "You disloyal little street rats. You would have nothing without the Wharf Man."

"We don't have much with him anyway," Aya replied. "And you seem to forget, Alton, that you and Oniel were street rats too. Just like us. Fighting to survive. Before you let the Wharf Man fill your heads with malice and evil. Now you are just his puppets."

That seemed to strike a nerve with Alton and he got in Aya's face. "Get out of the way."

"No," she said, standing her ground. "Not until you and your brother start thinking for yourselves and see that the Wharf Man isn't good for any of us. This is our chance to do something better. To go somewhere better. Far away from where he can reach us. You still have a chance. You and Oniel can find real peace."

Alton didn't speak and Purdue hoped that maybe her argument was sinking in. Whoever Alton and Oniel were before the Wharf Man ... maybe that part of them could be reached, and they could be reasoned with. Maybe those 'street rats' could be swayed away from the enforcers that they had become.

"Fine then," Alton said.

For a moment, everything fell silent. Everyone stood in shock that Alton was relenting. Aya's words had worked. Alton looked at his brother and nodded. Oniel nodded back, and to everyone's horror, moved forward with the knife still in his grasp, ready to start tabbing the crew one by one until he got to Purdue.

The twins were going to kill them all for their betrayal of the Wharf Man.

Purdue looked down at the pile of gold beside him. An old sword gleamed among the jewelry and trophies—an old scimitar that had probably been taken when Admiral Ogden's ships were out in the waters of the Middle East.

Purdue reached for it, wrapping his hand around the hilt and pulled the curved blade from the heap of treasure. He lunged forward through his group of supporters to protect them. Oniel retreated a few steps, and he glared at Purdue's sword. His little knife couldn't contend with a blade like that.

The crew took advantage of his hesitation and rushed Oniel like an angry mob. They swarmed him, forcing the knife from his hand. The blade skittered across the rocky terrain and the group piled on top of their enemy.

Alton fell back a short ways to avoid getting caught in the wave of arms and pulled a sword from another hill of treasure. It was a more traditional cutlass that he gave a few practices swipes with, before he moved to help his brother.

Purdue intercepted him, swinging the scimitar wildly and forcing Alton to defend himself, drawing his attention away from aiding Oniel. Their swords clashed together over and over. Purdue didn't have much skill with a sword, and the scimitar wasn't made for the little fencing knowledge he had. It wasn't meant for lunging and jabs. It was more of hacking and slashing kind of a weapon, but it would have to do in a duel.

It was clear that Alton wasn't a trained swordsman either, but his ferocity seemed to make up for it. He forced Purdue backward, moving up the slope of one of the golden mountains. As they dueled, the terrain they were on collapsed and slid under them. Coins rolled and splashed with each step while they reached the summit of one of the piles.

They must have been fighting for only a minute or two but Purdue was already exhausted. Every move at any second could have meant death. Sword duels looked so easy in the movies but those actors were just tapping their blunt props together. They weren't really trying to parry away killing strokes. They didn't have to worry that the blade was going to find its mark.

Alton might have been an amateur with a sword but he was an expert in combat otherwise. His general prowess in delivering violence was giving him the edge he needed in the duel. Purdue was barely keeping up and each moment that passed wore him down even more.

Alton threw his leg forward, kicking gold coins high up into Purdue's face. It was only a second, but it caused just enough of a distraction for Alton to slam his shoulder against Purdue. Purdue lost his already unsteady footing and tumbled down the slope. He rolled right down to the bottom, and it hadn't been a soft descent. A small avalanche of treasure swept down in his wake as he tried to get back up.

His opponent stood at the peak, laughing with the same arrogance that he usually let out. Purdue pulled himself up and glanced to his side to see how the crew was doing with Oniel. They were still wrestling with him, but he was putting up an impressive fight despite being so heavily outnumbered.

"This does not need to be hard," Alton called down. "Let it happen. Do not let it happen. It does not matter. It will still come to be either way."

Purdue brushed himself off, hoping Alton couldn't see the sweat pouring down his face. "You sound real sure of yourself, but I've hardly been trying." It was a bold-faced lie, but Purdue knew that half of a fight was all about how you presented yourself to your enemy. He needed to display resilience and strength. He pointed his scimitar up at Alton. "So are we done dancing around yet?"

Alton's face twisted into a mix of surprise and irritation. His expression hardened into a leer almost resembled his brother's perfectly. He was angry, and wanted this whole mess cleaned up immediately. To him, the best place to start cleaning up was with ending Purdue.

Alton jumped forward and slid down the mound of gold like it was a ski slope. The momentum from his slide launched him at Purdue, and Alton used that inertia to start an even more vicious series of strikes. Their swords clanged together rapidly, forcing Purdue farther back.

Alton wasn't holding back anymore. His swipes were laced with rage and were becoming harder and harder for Purdue to anticipate. He was barely keeping up at all now. He managed to block one swing only to have Alton throw a punch with his free hand. His knuckles smashed against Purdue's jaw, sending him reeling back. He managed to stay on his feet, but just barely.

Alton kept on him, not giving him a moment to get his bearings. His annoyance was emanating off him, and Purdue could practically feel his murderous intent backing his every attack.

Purdue was being pushed back toward the crew, who were still grappling with Oniel. If Alton got closer, he would probably start cutting them down. Purdue tried to hold him at bay and far away from his vulnerable allies. They had enough to deal with in their attempts to subdue Oniel.

However, he was hit again by a punch from Alton's free hand. It connected with the side of his head and Purdue fell onto his back. The whole world was spinning and throbbing. Or maybe that was his racing heartbeat. He wasn't sure. He just felt pain and fatigue weighing down on him, and keeping him from getting back up.

Alton stood over him and chuckled. "You took a fall, my friend."

Purdue desperately swiped at him from where he lay but

Alton easily deflected his strikes. Purdue shuffled backward on the ground, trying to crawl away and recover his footing, but Alton followed closely. He was very visibly relishing the sight of Purdue trying so hard to survive. That broad smile of his had never seemed bigger.

His cutlass smashed against Purdue's sword hard enough that it batted the scimitar out of his hand and flying into one of the mounds of treasure. Purdue toppled back onto his back, completely disarmed and now defenseless.

"You should have just accepted your role. Accepted whatever we gave you. Now this is just a mess. A mess that I have to clean up." Alton let out a sigh and pointed his sword at the crew nearby. "You know we are going to have to kill them now. All of them. That is on you. The Wharf Man does not tolerate insubordination and you made them all start talking crazy. You poisoned their minds. Gave them hopes for something that they can't have. You're going to be the one killing them. Not me. Not really."

"That's a load of shit," Purdue said, trying to pull himself backward on the ground, away from the sword pointing down at him. As his hands touched the ground, he felt something smooth graze against his fingers. He reached around some more to find that it was a knife—the one Oniel dropped when the crew jumped him. "If anyone's mind is poisoned, it's you and your brother. The rest of the crew just understands that they could have a better life than running errands for a goddamn vulture like the Wharf Man."

"Quiet!" Alton barked.

Purdue slowly wrapped his hand around the handle of Oniel's knife behind his back.

"You should have just known your place. You are already a dead man, hmm? Is that not what you told us? So there is really no harm in killing you again, is there?"

It sounded quite harmful actually.

Purdue tightened his grip on the knife behind him, making sure he had a good hold of it. It could make all the difference.

Alton looked happy to have Purdue looking up at him like he was superior. He kept inching closer with his sword, taking full advantage of the situation. "I will tell the Wharf Man that you thanked him for all of the help he gave you. You were so grateful, weren't you?"

Alton raised his sword for the killing blow. It was a split second delay, but it had to be enough. It had to. Purdue launched himself forward, throwing his whole body at his opponent. He kept Oniel's knife in front of him, and as their bodies collided, the small blade sank into Alton's chest. Alton looked down at Purdue with wide eyes, and a weak gasp left his mouth. He trembled and stared at the knife piercing his heart. His sword fell from his hand and clattered on the ground. Purdue was practically embracing him, with one hand on his back and the other still clutching the knife that found its target.

As dangerous as Alton was, Purdue never wanted their

alliance to end like this. He would have preferred some-thing peaceful; an amicable end after staying true to the deal that was initially made. Instead, Alton had a blade in him and was choking on his own blood, just like Purdue would have been.

Purdue really needed to stop making deals with such dangerous individuals. It never panned out well for him in the end. It usually ended with betrayal, attempted murder, and with Purdue feeling like a gullible moron.

Alton crumbled downward and Purdue crouched along with him. Alton's eyes kept fluttering as his life slipped away. He leaned in close, resting his chin on Purdue's shoulder.

The dying man whispered in his ear. "My ... my brother will ... kill you..."

The more jovial of the murderous twins choked out one final laugh before falling permanently silent, almost as silent as his living brother.

Purdue let Alton slip off of him and slump onto the ground, dead.

Oniel let out a horrible, hollow shout of rage from behind Purdue. He started pushing and bashing the crew out of his way. His attention was fixed on Purdue and Alton's body. He shoved anyone who tried to stop him away, and started advancing on Purdue. He was filled with utter fury, and was going to rip Purdue to pieces for what he'd done.

Purdue picked up the cutlass Alton had dropped and prepared to defend himself, but there was no need. Aya appeared behind Oniel, catching up behind him, and hit him in the back of the head with a jewelry box she had plucked out of the piles of treasure. Oniel dropped hard, tipping over like a seven foot tree. He lay unconscious near his dead brother. Purdue looked down to see the same face on two bodies, both with their eyes closed. One was still gently breathing, while the other never would again.

He looked up from the twins to Aya and smiled. "Thanks."

Aya nodded, dropping the jewelry box and pointing at Oniel. "What do we do with him now?"

It was a good question. He was a threat to them, and the moment he was awake, he would surely come after them to avenge his fallen brother. But, Purdue was in no mood to have to kill someone else. One was hard enough, no matter how evil the victim was.

"We'll tie him up and decide later."

"We should kill him!" Jermaine shouted out, earning many nods of approval from the crew. "He will hunt us all down for this. And he loves tracking people down. He is good at it. He will find us all and we will all be dead. The Wharf Man will be bad enough. Oniel is crazy and will make sure we all have our throats slit by the end."

"We have other things we need to focus on right now,"

Purdue said. "Like getting the gold out of here. We can't fit all of this onto the boats."

"No, we cannot," Aya agreed. "Perhaps we should leave some behind. Surely we do not need it all."

Purdue shook his head. His future was going to be full of challenges against an enemy with an incredible amount of resources. The full amount of treasure was only a start to begin with. He couldn't do with even less than that. "I need all of it that I can spare. Especially since I am giving much of it to all of you."

"But without the percentage you were going to give to the Wharf Man—"

"I need it," Purdue said firmly. And he certainly did need it.

Every coin would matter in his battle to reclaim his life from the Order of the Black Sun.

The group discussed many possible strategies to transport the treasure, but none of the ideas they came up with seemed feasible. Jermaine even suggested that they haul much of it behind the ship in a trawling net. That wasn't the brightest idea Purdue had ever heard.

"This is impossible," Aya said after hearing enough genius ideas. "There is no way we can take it all in one boat."

Something occurred to Purdue.

"Wait a minute." He was angry that the thought hadn't

crossed his mind earlier. It would have saved them all quite a bit of time. "We won't have to."

Aya looked at him with bewilderment. "I do not understand."

"We don't need to take it all off of the island. We just need to convince the Wharf Man that we have. We can take as much as we can, and then bury the rest."

"Leave it here?" Aya asked. "We cannot do that. If the Wharf Man comes ... or if someone else comes..."

"The Wharf Man will come," Purdue said certainly. "I'll make sure he does."

The crew all looked at one another nervously, like Purdue had lost his mind.

"He's coming either way. I'm sure Alton gave him the coordinates to this place. So let him come. He won't be looking very hard for the treasure if he thinks it's all gone."

The cogs turning in Aya's head were almost visible as she put the pieces of Purdue's new plan together. She realized exactly what he meant, and her lips almost formed into an uncertain smile.

Burying most of the treasure and hoping the Wharf Man didn't notice. It wasn't the best plan, and might not even be a good one, but it was the best chance anyone could think of to protect it. It would be right underneath the Wharf Man's nose, underneath his feet even, but he wouldn't see it. He'd be too angry that his prize had been taken. And Purdue would leave Oniel behind to further distract the Wharf Man. He would make for a good mocking consolation prize.

"It could work," Purdue said. "Let's play pirate and bury some treasure."

11

THE TRUE TREASURE

P urdue strolled through the cavern that housed the treasure, taking a quiet moment to appreciate just how many plundered prizes were around him. Even with a whole fleet at his disposal, it was still incredible that Admiral Ogden was able to amass such a vast amount of gold.

There were currency and valuable trinkets from all different parts of the world, evidence of just how far Admiral Ogden's fleet had traveled the seas. No other pirates probably operated in so many of the world's seas. Their spoils of war were trophies from all over. Few places hadn't at least felt the threat of Admiral Ogden's fleet at one point or another.

Chests were filled with coin with all kinds of designs and numerous languages on them. Most of these treasure chests were massive and almost overflowing with gold.

One chest, however, particularly stood out among all of the others. It was a small box made of wood and didn't seem like it could fit much gold at all inside. A far cry from the trunks brimming with sparkling wealth. It looked like it didn't belong with its far shinier surroundings. It was a blemish on the beautiful, gleaming pile of treasure.

Out of curiosity, Purdue crouched down to the small chest and picked it up, nonchalantly popping it open. There wasn't more coin inside. There wasn't an antique dagger or some stolen jewelry. The only thing inside was an old, torn up book.

Purdue almost shut the chest immediately. Given everything that happened with Mona Greer's book of shadows, he knew better now than to mess with dusty tomes. Who knew was horrible things were written inside of it?

He hesitated a moment before shutting it, because he got a different feeling from this book than he had gotten from that book of shadows in Salem. Firstly, this book wasn't emanating with the same unsettling aura as that spell book had been. Whatever was inscribed on these pages, they couldn't be worse than what was in the book of shadows. That was highly unlikely.

Purdue took the book out of the little chest. It was messily bound together and its condition hadn't been helped by its time sitting in a cave for hundreds of years.

Purdue fought through his nervousness and immediately realized he was holding a journal. As he read on, it became clear that the book wasn't just any journal either. It was Admiral Ogden's personal log book. The entries were overall short but filled with interesting and exciting information. It recounted the *Scarlet Wing's* location on various dates, depicted exploits that the crew committed —both good and bad—and best of all, gave insight into Admiral Ogden's thoughts on everything that was happening back then.

It was easy for Purdue to skim through it, knowing that he would be giving it a much more thorough read soon enough. He would be pouring many hours reading something like that. Now that he was on his way to having money again, hopefully he would be reading it from a comfortable home, or from in his bath tub.

He skipped ahead to the last page of the log that had anymore writing on it. It was about halfway through the remaining pages, like the author had given up half way through, or maybe he was forced to.

The journal entry written on that final page answered some of those questions.

Admiral Walton Ogden wrote:

If there is a soul reading this, then that soul has found what I have left behind. My log book will be included with all of the riches that I have and my extensive crew have acquired over the course of my life. I am uncertain as to how much of this gold will be present when my journal is found. I am in the midst of making preparations for the largest venture that we have taken part in. We will soon be attacking a Spanish galleon that could potentially double the amount of gold that I currently possess. You, reading this, will certainly know the answer better than I.

The truth of all of this is something I have even withheld from my own crew, men who I have long considered family. So many of them think that I have such glorious plans for everything we have taken. They believe that all of our stealing and raiding will have some true meaning in the world. They are mistaken, I'm afraid, and I do not have the heart to tell them that.

I have nothing planned for this gold. Some days I do not even know why I took it to begin with or why I still desire more. I have been unable to stop myself from just trying to get as much as I can, damn the consequences. I have no idea what I want all of this for, or what real need I have of it. I am one of the wealthiest men in the world now, but there is nothing I want to do with that wealth, except to get more of it.

Hopefully, if you have found it, you have loftier aspirations than I do. I pray that you are not stricken with this unshakable avarice that I have been long suffering from. Someday, perhaps even soon, that greed will get me killed. I am sure of it.

My gold, my legacy, now belongs to you.

Purdue thought that those words seemed like the end of the message that Admiral Ogden left behind, but the pirate continued for half a page longer.

It read: *Know this. I have put everything I ever collected* as a pirate in this cave. *Everything except one particular piece of treasure. It is not among the piles of gold that you have found. It was too dangerous to have. Most things I found at sea were material. They were belongings that I could take and understand the value of. This treasure was not so simplistic, but it was valuable in an altogether different way. This item could control the very sea itself, far too dangerous for a rum-soaked man like myself to have.*

Much like my gold, and like any good pirate worth his name, I buried it.

Though I did not bury it in sand and stone. I buried it where it belonged. At sea. That is where it no doubt still rests, far away from the reach of man.

To fully accept my legacy, then you must find my final treasure, but remember that it is not as simple as gold. Search for it at your own peril.

Spend wisely.

Signed, Admiral Walton Ogden.

Purdue practically dropped the logbook. There was some secret power that Admiral Ogden dropped into the ocean, something so powerful that even a warrior of the sea like him was too afraid to even hold onto it, and this was a man who horded everything he ever took. As valuable and useful as all of this was to him, maybe that was the kind of power he needed to really get his life back. Maybe that was the secret weapon that could literally turn the tides against the Order of the Black Sun.

Purdue took the logbook and tucked it under his coat, as his crew came down to the cavern to begin their plan to hide the treasure from its initial resting place. As much as they had earned his trust and he now even considered some his friends, the captain's log book should remain in the hands of the captain, and not his crew.

———————

Purdue and the crew got to work digging an enormous hole to move the treasure into. They split up into shifts where some got the treasure prepared for transport, while others devoted all of their time and energy to digging. It was long and challenging project, but all working together, they started to chip away at the enormous task in front of them.

They made sure to keep all of their digging out of sight of the enemies that they had tied up—Oniel, and Luka's pirates. They couldn't risk having them see the new hiding place for the gold. If their plan worked and the Wharf Man really did come to try and find it, they couldn't have any of their prisoners knowing that the treasure was still on the island, just out of the cavern. They even made a point of lugging some gold past where they were being held, just to make it look like they were taking it all away. The Wharf Man needed to believe, without a reasonable doubt, that they had somehow absconded with every single coin.

It took some time, but after loading a good portion of it onto the ship, they dumped the rest into the pit they had created and then got to work filling it in and making it look as undisturbed as they could. Ideally, the Wharf Man would walk across that piece of land, directly above what he was after, and have no idea that he had missed it.

It was risky, but Purdue believed it was the only way. The treasure needed to be protected, and giving it up for a time might be the best way to do that.

12

WHAT THE MUTE HAS TO SAY

I f Oniel wasn't restrained, they would probably have all been dead. He sat quietly, a rope wrapped tightly around his arms and torso, against a large palm tree. Luka and the remaining members of his pirate crew were tied to their own trees nearby. Oniel stared blankly at the crew from where he was stuck. He was probably imagining hundreds of ways to tear all of them apart. To bath himself in their blood and dance on their remains on the ground.

Alton's body was nearby, but the crew had the decency to cover it with a blanket from the boat, so Oniel didn't have to look at his brother's corpse. Seeing your brother dead was bad enough. But seeing your identical twin brother's lifeless body must have been torturous. You would know exactly what you would look like dead. You would see yourself as a corpse. In some respects, you would be attending your very own funeral.

Luka and his few remaining pirates were constantly shouting nearby, cursing Purdue and threatening that they would someday get him back for everything that had been done. Purdue wasn't afraid of them. They were just scavengers, and they knew just as well as he did, that if the Wharf Man came and found them there, he would probably send their heads back to his rival and their boss, Siad. Purdue hoped that the missing treasure would be enough to infuriate the Wharf Man, and that his rivals' presence would be enough to distract him from thinking too much about where the treasure could have gone. He could take his anger out on them, and let that fury cloud his thoughts.

Purdue walked up to his silent prisoner tied to the tree and was relieved Oniel was mute. It saved them the trouble of having to bind his mouth if he started complaining or cursing at them like Luka and his men were doing. On the other hand, sitting there still and silent made him almost invisible. He was a predator just watching and waiting for an opening to strike.

Oniel looked at him with the same disdain that he always had, but now there was real hatred mixed in. Of everyone, Oniel undoubtedly hated Purdue the most for killing Alton. And of all the numerous ways Oniel could imagine that he would kill the crew, he was assuredly saving the worst of them for Purdue.

"I didn't want to do it, you know," Purdue said honestly, leaning forward to almost be eye level with Alton. "Killing Alton. It's not what I wanted. It never was. You and your brother didn't give me much of a choice, though, did you? You were going to kill me and everyone else, just for disagreeing with you. That kind of attitude was bound to cause some friction, aye?"

Oniel didn't answer, not even with his face. He looked away from Purdue to the sand beneath him. Nothing Purdue said would matter. The only thing that mattered to Oniel now was slaughtering the people who took his brother from him.

"You were going to kill us, all of us, for disobeying a man who tore out your tongue. A man who you are still loyal to even after he did that."

Oniel's gaze remained averted to the ground.

"We're going to be taking the treasure. All of it. In a little while, I'm going to tell the Wharf Man where to find us. By the time he gets here, we'll be gone with the treasure. But maybe he'll pick you up. Hopefully he'll get here before you starve or dehydrate or whatever. That would be a shame. And hopefully before your brother rots too much."

This brought Oniel's attention back. He looked up at Purdue with those blank, murderous eyes and made some sounds for the first time. Grunts and gargles as he opened his mouth. Purdue leaned in close to hear the noise.

"Ki ... oo ... ki ... oo."

The sounds that left Oniel's mouth were hoarse, but Purdue could hear the words that he was trying to form.

He could hear them clearly, and the message that they sent rang even more clearly.

'Kill you.'

Purdue rose back up. "Oh yeah? From there? Do it then. Half the crew thinks we should just get rid of you now. Hell, maybe we should. It would ensure that you never bothered anyone again."

Oniel's scornful gaze kept boring into him.

"But I won't," Purdue said. "Like I said, I didn't want it to be like this. I didn't want to kill Alton. I don't want to kill you. Do you deserve it? Yeah. You probably do, but that's not for me to decide. At least you'll have a fighting chance tied to this tree rather than in the ground."

If the Wharf Man didn't come, then Oniel would slowly die over the course of a few days. Was it right to leave him behind to slowly perish? Probably not, but it was the best Purdue would for a monster like him. It was more merciful than he deserved.

Purdue walked away and when he glanced over his shoulder, Oniel was still sitting there quietly, staring at Purdue. Purdue didn't know what was to come, but he had a horrible feeling that he would see those same eyes again, with just as much anger behind them.

13

THE END OF THE BUSINESS ARRANGEMENT

Purdue took a seat on a long piece of driftwood that was washed up on the beach. He started out at the horizon at everything that was out there, unseen. He was so far way form it all. From the Wharf Man. From the Order of the Black Sun. From the life that used to be his, practically a cast away from his own past.

But now it was becoming a little more clear. He was sitting on the fortune that would begin his redemption. It wasn't time yet, though. Now he needed to confront the man who had tried to stab him in the back.

Purdue held up Alton's radio and clicked it on, listening to the static and crackling before speaking into it.

"Beautiful day, isn't it?"

Delroy Campbell was a patient man. He always prided himself on being that way. It was the only way to live. It was best to take things slow, and allow things to slowly gravitate around you until they were within reach. It was always inevitable that something would come your way. There was no need to rush it. It would come in time. So he constantly found himself waiting. Waiting for others to come to him, with their ideas and their proposals and even their threats. He waited until his gravity was too much; he could pull them in enough so that they wouldn't ever escape.

Delroy Campbell was a smart man. He was always told so by his peers. Part of that was because of the patience that he was so proud of. His patience gave him enough time to think clearly, and when he was thinking clearly, no one could be smarter than him. They couldn't see things the way he could. They couldn't see the potential like he could. He always saw what others couldn't. That's what made him smart. He wasn't a scientist. He wasn't a mathematician. He was smart because he knew things that others didn't. He was smart because others trusted his word and his knowledge, even when it wasn't entirely accurate. He may not have been smart in the eyes of scholars or historians, but in the eyes and minds of those who bowed before him, he was the smartest man there ever was.

Delroy Campbell was most importantly a powerful man. Everyone knew it, all across the oceans. They knew that he was the one who made all of the decisions. It didn't matter who you were, whether it was a politician, a soldier, a police officer, or even just a tree trimmer, they all recognized the power he possessed. It was different than most power. It wasn't given to him or trusted to him. He took it for himself, and he made it grow. It was still growing. He was considered a big man, but not just for his size, but for the shadow that he cast over everything and anything that happened in Jamaica and throughout the Caribbean.

Delroy Campbell was all of these things—patient, smart, and powerful—and that was what made him the Wharf Man.

So Delroy sat at his desk, listening to updates about all of his business dealings. From the drug running, to the human trafficking, to the racketeering. His business was frowned upon and even illegal, but no one dared try to stop him. They all knew their place. They knew not to get in the way of the Wharf Man's dealings. It was a wonderful thing to be that feared, but it also made things boring at times, and as he listened to each one, he realized that it wasn't the pieces of business he wanted to hear most.

All of those things he was being told were so normal. They were his everyday money. They were the way that he controlled things. They were the very fabric of the web he weaved throughout the entire island. They were the usual fair.

The only piece of business he really had a current interest in was the one that he had heard nothing about since it started. Since he last saw that broke ass billionaire sail off on one of his boats. That David Purdue, promising him a cut of an old pirate's treasure. It was an exciting deal, if only to see if there was actually any truth to it all. Delroy hoped there was, because if there was, he wasn't going to be settling for any measly thirty percent. A man of his status didn't settle for that, especially not when it was being offered by a poor man with nothing left to his name.

Still, that David Purdue did get him thinking. He got him thinking a lot actually. He was a fascinating man to do business with because he literally had nothing else left to lose. It had all been taken by some enemy that he was mysteriously vague about. Some secret society of rich people in Europe or something, it didn't matter to Delroy. The only thing that mattered to him was the here and now.

The past meant nothing, that's what David Purdue—Mr. Yesterday—didn't understand.

If the past mattered, then Delroy would still just be a big, plump boy begging for scraps, begging for work, and begging for some love. He would still be beat by his father and shamed by his mother. He would still be getting his ass beat every day.

It was all different now. The past made no difference anymore. He might as well have been a different person, and in a way he was. The Wharf Man's name was one he wasn't very happy with at first. It didn't quite have the intensity that he would like to give off. Slowly, however, he came around to it, when he saw just how much fear it put into the people on his island. It was simple enough that it left them guessing at what exactly he was.

And now—now it was the only name they knew him by.

Delroy Campbell was a name that had been forgotten on the island. The ones who knew it never spoke it anymore. The Wharf Man had become synonymous with Jamaica. He was probably the most famous man in the whole country, but he wasn't on the front page of the newspaper or the cover of a magazine. The Wharf Man was famous, but no one cheered his name. He was a man of whispers and rumors. The wise man people would come to when they needed help, his guidance, or a favor.

Just like David Purdue had. He had heard that name— the Wharf Man. He had coming looking for him, to help dig him out of the grave that he was going to be buried in, if he didn't get his life back together. And Delroy, being a patient man, listened to Purdue's request for aid. And being a smart man, he considered what a deal with a man like David Purdue could bring. And being a powerful man, he decided that David Purdue would find that treasure, and he would give all of it to him or die.

If that treasure did exist, it belonged the Wharf Man.

Beside him, his radio started to crackle, and he hushed his subordinates telling him about the day's events. Their bullshit about some of their drugs being stolen would have to wait. Those girls on the sidewalk would have to wait. All of his usual business would have to wait because finally, after a long damn time, he was going to hear an update about the business he really cared about.

He'd given that radio to Alton to contact him once the treasure was found and not a moment before. He didn't want to hear anyone on that boat until they brought good news, not since he learned about the island actually existing. So the frequency coming in meant that the treasure was found. He expected Alton's joyful excitement to come through the crackles in the speaker. Instead, he heard another voice altogether.

It was Mr. Yesterday.

"Beautiful day, isn't it?"

Purdue stared at the radio in his hand. There was nothing for some time. A minute went by. Then maybe two or three minutes passed. It felt much longer to him, as he listened to the static.

The Wharf Man's voice boomed through the speaker. "It warms my heart to hear from you, Mr. Yesterday. I had feared the worst. How goes the preparations with the gold? Alton told me that you had found the island you believed it to be on."

Purdue answered with a blunt retort. "It could have gone better."

The radio was quiet again. The Wharf Man was probably waiting for Purdue's submission to the altered deal the twins had presented him. He probably thought that was the only possible reason for Purdue contacting him— a surrender—but Purdue wouldn't give him one. Not ever.

"Things took a bit of a hard turn when your men tried to kill me and the rest of the crew."

A tangible awkwardness hung between the call, felt all the way across the ocean in the incredible distance between the two men, stretching miles and miles. It was Purdue's turn to wait for a response.

Finally one came when the Wharf Man let out a deep laugh. "You must be joking. What happened?"

Purdue gripped the radio tighter. The nerve of the Wharf Man ... the sheer arrogance to play dumb and laugh when he knew exactly why the twins had tried to kill Purdue. It was the same reason that Alton and Oniel had done anything in their lives—because the Wharf Man said to.

Purdue decided to just spell it out for his enemy. "Alton decided that all of the gold was yours and offered a new arrangement. That I shut my mouth and let you take it all. I politely refused the new deal. He got angry. Harsh words were said." Purdue let the suspense linger. He made the Wharf Man wait before getting to the end. "So I stabbed him in the heart."

The Wharf Man didn't bother with the silence this time. His response was immediate, and stunned. "You ... you did what?"

"Don't sound so surprised," Purdue said. "He was seconds away from doing the same to me. All because you had your own plans to break our deal."

Purdue felt his anger rising through his body. He wanted to yell and swear at this bastard for his treachery but he kept himself relatively composed. Watching the tides roll in on the beach helped sooth him enough to stay in check.

"Where is Oniel?" The Wharf Man asked, not denying the accusation of his involvement.

"That guy?" Purdue laughed and made sure that the Wharf Man heard it. "He's fine for now. I haven't quite decided what to do with him yet. Given his lack of a tongue, you obviously believe in strong punishments. So what do you suggest I do with someone like him? Same thing I did to his brother?"

"You will not touch him. You will not dare." The Wharf Man was clearly rattled, and Purdue was beginning to understand just how strong of a pressure point he was pressing down on. The twins were practically sons to the crime boss. The Wharf Man may have been tough, but this was hurting him.

Purdue continued. "I thought we had an understanding. No backstabbing, remember? You kept saying that. Not to break the deal and no turning on one another. No backstabbing! None! So tell me why the hell I feel like I'm pulling a knife out of my back right now? You get thirty percent. That was the deal we had. Then I'm hearing that you're actually getting one hundred percent and I should just be happy about it."

That deep laugh returned through the radio.

"It was my boat. And my crew."

"We had a deal," Purdue maintained. "You didn't stick to it. So I don't have to anymore either."

"What do you mean by that?"

"I mean the second you broke the deal, you forfeited any and all claim you had on the treasure." Purdue spoke the coordinates of the island. It felt strange in a way, to be giving away their location, but it was part of the plan that was brewing in his head. "You're welcome to come see for yourself, but you won't find much of anything. I'm taking it all. Every last coin. Come have a look ... and hell, maybe I'll leave Oniel here for you to pick up as a parting gift. You may not get any of the spoils but at least you'll have your boy back, aye? Oh, and I forgot to mention, your friend Siad has some pirates, aye? Well some of them came after us. There are a few here waiting for you as well. Another parting gift. Never say I never got you anything."

"Think carefully about this," the Wharf Man said, sounding uneasy.

"Oh, I have. Very carefully."

"That crew ... my crew ... they will not stand for this. They won't let you—"

"They already have," Purdue said. "And they don't work for you anymore, by the way. They don't need your hand-outs or your leftovers. They're done groveling at your feet for crumbs."

The Wharf Man's rage simmered through the radio. He was a volcano on the verge of erupting. "You will not do this."

"It's being done right now. We're taking it all." It was a lie but it felt good to know that it was making the Wharf Man squirm.

The Wharf Man laughed again but there was no joy or amusement in it this time. Just pure, seething malice. He was a spoiled child who was being denied something for the first time. The big baby was ready to throw a tantrum.

"You are stealing from me, hmm? From me."

"Not really," Purdue said. "This gold was never yours and you tried to steal it from me first. So..."

"You will die for this," the Wharf Man interrupted, on the brink of exploding. "You hear me? I will find you, wherever you go. You will die when I do. You understand me? Do you understand me?!"

"I understand," Purdue said casually. "Good luck finding me. In the meantime, I'll enjoy *my* treasure."

The Wharf Man's booming chuckle echoed once more, full of contempt and disbelief that someone was standing against his might.

"There will be no tomorrow for you, Mr. Yesterday. No tomorrow."

Purdue clicked the radio off and let the sound of breaking waves flush out the threat that still lingered in the air.

Someone he hoped would be a powerful ally against the Black Sun was officially an enemy. He should have never worked with someone like the Wharf Man to begin with. And he should have especially never trusted him to keep his word.

At least his crew turned out far more reliable than their boss. Money may have been their only motivation, but that's how it was for most people in the world. Now it was that way for Purdue too. He needed money just like anyone else, and maybe with the information he had about Ogden's last missing treasure, he could get something even better than wealth.

It would be his next venture, and he just needed a crew. Hopefully, he already had one.

―――――

Delroy Campbell was a patient man, but now he lost his patience.

Delroy Campbell was a smart man, who had just been outmaneuvered.

Delroy Campbell was a powerful man, who had just been made powerless.

All because of David Purdue.

The Wharf Man let out a thunderous roar and flipped the desk in front of him. The few lieutenants he had in the room flinched and some even backed toward the door. They had seen their boss upset before, and they knew that his rampages could often end with blood and broken bones. Being anywhere near him in that state was like standing in front of a hurricane or a stampede of elephants. There was a high chance it was going to end badly.

The conversation played back in his head, and he had never had one like it before. For the first time, someone actually believed they could rip him off. Purdue really thought that he was going to get away with this, but he wouldn't. The Wharf Man would find him, drag him back to the shores of Jamaica, and tear out his spine just to show the world what happened to a man who thought that he was better than him. No one had ever spoken to him that way before. That arrogant Scottish bastard got one taste of wealth again and already he thought he was superior.

Not only that, but he murdered Alton, a boy who Delroy had raised. A boy who was, in everything but genetics, his son. Purdue took him. He took his life. No one was supposed to take anything from the Wharf Man. Anyone who did would suffer for it, and Purdue would certainly suffer.

"Sir," one of his men, Fitzroy, said, slowly approaching. "Are you good?"

"Good?" The Wharf Man sneered. "Do I look good, Fitzroy? We have been robbed. He robbed us! He took Alton. He took Oniel. He took the crew. He took the gold! He took everything! After I gave him a ship and a crew, he stole from me!"

He was in a blind rage, one so severe that he could barely see the room around him. All he saw was that smug Scotsman who came crawling for help and now took from him.

And that crew, Aya and her sailors, they had betrayed him too. That was even worse than Purdue. He was an outsider who could be excused for not being aware of how things worked in Jamaica, but Aya ... beautiful Aya ... she should have known better. She did know better. And yet she betrayed him all the same. She would have to die first. He would make sure Purdue and her whole crew watched when he took her life. She had sworn loyalty to him like anyone else and had turned out to be nothing more than a rat.

They all thought they were going to be rich, no doubt. They thought David Purdue would give them a better offer. Perhaps he would, maybe he was really going to give them some of the treasure, but they should have realized that no amount of riches would matter if they betrayed the Wharf Man, because they would have no chance to even spend it. He would find them all, and he would make sure they remembered who they really worked for, before he fired them from his employment in the most brutal of ways. They were all treacherous fools who thought that they had a real choice. They wouldn't for long.

And Oniel—poor, quiet, Oniel—he had been tough on him, he would admit. Tearing his tongue from his mouth was undeniably the right thing to do at the time, but there were times when he missed his laughs. Unlike Alton, Oniel didn't try and pretend to be anything but what he really was, a killer bred to serve the Wharf Man. That was what he had raised those twin brothers to be. And while Oniel let his tongue get the better of him once, he was an even more efficient killer than his brother. As many liked to point out, Alton was the one that would stab you in the front. Oniel was the one that would stab you many times in the back. And now, that powerful duo, his right and left hands, had been divided.

He would never hear Alton's advice again. He would never be able to watch that boy carry out his orders with such swift severity, and sometimes showmanship. He would have to settle for Oniel's quiet, understated ability to complete tasks. That was, if he could rescue him from that godforsaken island.

"You took down those coordinates?" The Wharf Man barked.

"I did," Fitzroy stammered and handed him a slip of paper with them on it. "Exactly as he said."

"Good," the Wharf Man mused, looking it over. "Get a ship prepared. We're going there immediately."

"Why?" Fitzroy asked. "Didn't he say he took the treasure? We really going to go all that way for that lunatic, Oniel—?"

The Wharf Man grabbed Fitzroy by the face and squeezed down on his jawline. Fitzroy gasped and tried to pry the Wharf Man's hands off, but his boss far outweighed him in the realms of power. He could pop his head like a cherry if he really wanted to. The Wharf Man took a hold of Fitzroy's tongue, pinching down on it. Fitzroy had tears in his eyes, remembering exactly what happened to someone who spoke when they shouldn't.

"Yes," the Wharf Man said quietly. "We are going there for Oniel. Unlike you, Fitzroy, he has helped me many times over the years and we are going to reward him for his loyalty. Perhaps as a special gift, I will even give him your tongue to replace the one he's lost. He has earned it back, wouldn't you say?"

The Wharf Man relished the bloodshot fear in Fitzroy's eyes. That was the power that he could wield. It wasn't his physical strength that was scaring his subordinate. It was the fact that Fitzroy knew the Wharf Man could decide his fate with the flick of his risk, with a snap of his fingers, or with a single word. He could erase him from the world with a thought.

"P-p-please," Fitzroy managed through the fingers that were clenching his face. "I'm. I'm sorry."

"I know you are," the Wharf Man said and pinched a little harder. "But you know I have to do this."

"N-no! Plea—"

The Wharf Man pulled hard and Fitzroy let out a terrible shriek. The other lieutenants in the room all averted their eyes. None of them wanted to risk even looking at the Wharf Man in a way he might find insulting. The Wharf Man dropped Fitzroy to the ground, who was choking on his own blood and screaming. There was a possibility that he might not survive this injury, and the Wharf Man was always okay with that risk. If they did survive, like Oniel had, then that meant they still had some fight in them, and still some use to him.

"Yes we are going to go to that island. We're going to get Oniel off of there, and once we have him back, we are going to find David Purdue. We're going to find him and the crew he stole from me. We're going to kill them all one-by-one. Get every ship we have. I want every boat, every man, and we're going to find everyone that has stolen from me today. We will find them no matter where they hide, and we will make that man wish he never came to me for help."

His inner circle all nodded in approval and then left the room, partially to get to work as quickly as possible, but mostly just to get away from the madman who was their boss. Fitzroy held his mouth and practically crawled from the room, and the Wharf Man just watched as he slunk away like the worm he was.

Once he was alone again, the Wharf Man picked up his desk. It was far from the first time that he had thrown it to the floor. It had a number of dents and scratches from its frequent meetings with the floor. He straightened it back up and tidied up the counter top. Slowly, he lowered himself back down into his chair, which almost collapsed under his weight like usual. He sat there at his desk, and once again thought about all of the business he had to deal with.

Delroy Campbell was a patient man, when he managed to be.

Delroy Campbell was a smart man, when he could think clearly.

Delroy Campbell was a powerful man, when he made sure the world remembered it.

Delroy Campbell was the Wharf Man—and he never let anyone take from him.

14

A NEW HEADING

Purdue gathered the crew on the shore, the ocean becoming his backdrop.

"There is something you should all know about," Purdue said and held up the logbook of the late Admiral Ogden. "All of this treasure is incredible. Truly. But there was something left behind that might prove to be even more valuable than any amount of gold. Something else that Admiral Ogden left behind."

The crew all waited with bated breath to hear what he had to say. Some looked at the logbook uneasily, like they couldn't believe there was a prize better than the vast amounts of wealth they had uncovered in the cave on the island. What could be better than enough wealth to change their lives forever?

"In one of Admiral Ogden's entries, he mentions a true treasure—something one of a kind—that he had found.

He describes it as being something so powerful, that it would give the person who found it complete control of the sea. Ogden didn't want that. He didn't want that power. So he buried it somewhere so deep, that no one could ever find it."

"He buried more treasure?" Aya asked. "Didn't he already bury enough?"

"Unlike his gold, he didn't bury this in the ground. No. He buried this treasure at sea."

"How are we supposed to get that?" Aya asked. "I do not believe our boat can travel under the sea, can it? We could never reach it. Whatever it even is."

"I'm not sure about the specifics yet," Purdue said bluntly. "But it would be an expensive venture, I'm sure. Luckily, money is no longer an issue for us, is it?"

The crew all mumbled and nodded in agreement. They had just found so much gold, that nothing was really out of the realm of possibility. People had dived to the bottom of the ocean before. It was a possible journey, but they would need the proper vessel to get down there, and they must have had enough money to help make that possible now. With a fortune, there was no such thing as an impossibility; there were no limits to where you could reach.

"We will find a place to rest and recuperate from this journey," Purdue explained. "We will get all of our new found fortunes situated ... and then soon enough, we will start a new journey for anyone who is brave enough to join me. We will find the treasure that Admiral Ogden discarded and dropped in the sea, and if he was right, it will give us more power than we can imagine. Something even better than money."

It was hard to figure out an accurate estimate of the crew's response to the idea. Some seemed excited by the idea, while others looked at him with far more trepidation. He couldn't blame any who weren't interested. They barely survived this journey; who knew if they could survive a second. But then again, a trust had formed between him and the crew at this point. They no longer looked at him as the stranger from a foreign land who called the shots simply because the Wharf Man declared it. He had truly become their captain, and they respected him in that position now. Hell, they had even come to his aid against the twins, turning on people they once considered their superiors.

"It is entirely optional. I will respect any and all of your decisions, whatever those might be."

There were more little conversations among the crew and Aya stepped forward first. "You know I will join you on this. There is nothing for me back home but the Wharf Man's anger, and you have not led us astray so far. I look forward to seeing what this lost treasure of the admiral's really is. I will make sure that I do."

Purdue smiled and gave her an appreciative nod. Out of anyone else, she had proven herself to be the most trustworthy and loyal of the whole crew. She lived up to her title as his first mate in all respects, including inspiring the other members of the crew. Aya's words had struck a chord with the rest of them as well as they all, one-by-one, declared their intentions to join him on a trip to the bottom of the sea. Soon enough, the whole crew had pledged to join him on a second venture.

Purdue felt a wave of pride swoop over him.

Hopefully this new venture would go far better than their maiden voyage.

EPILOGUE

Purdue stared out at the sea from his penthouse. He never thought he'd have views from that high up ever again. He never thought he would be staying in such comfortable accommodations again either. He wouldn't take it for granted this time.

The ocean had given him a new lease on life. It had given him another chance, and with Admiral Ogden's log and the true treasure he talked about, then the seas might still be able to give him even more. This could be the final push he needed to move against the Order of the Black Sun. To not only take back what was rightfully his, but to save his friends and colleagues who had been abducted.

Maybe it was the comfortable bed, or maybe it was that he was finally able to shower, but David Purdue was feeling truly hopeful for the first time since losing everything.

"Look at you putting yourself back together," a voice said.

Purdue turned around suddenly and instinctively reached for anything he could use as a weapon to defend himself. He settled on a pen sitting on the table beside him. He had come too far to be found and killed now.

A woman stepped out of the darkness of the room and Purdue recognized her uptight expression immediately. It was Sasha, the agent of the Black Sun who had rescued him from that burning fire. He still didn't know why exactly. Just that she seemed to want Julian Corvus removed just as much as he did. He owed her his life, but he also owed her for helping those bastards burn down his home and take everything from him.

"Sasha..."

"You don't look happy to see me," Sasha said, not looking too happy herself.

"Surprised is the word I would use. Last time I saw you, you were pulling my ass from a fire and telling me to be dead. Well ... I've been dead. David Purdue is still supposed to be ash, with nothing but an empty grave and some tabloid rumors to leave behind."

"You have done well to stay hidden, I have to admit."

"Obviously, I haven't done a good enough job. You found me easily enough."

"That's because I'm the only one looking. The only one of the Black Sun who knows the truth. You're welcome by the way. Clever how you robbed that bank. Was that something from that spell book you found?"

Purdue nodded, but felt a little annoyed that she had been able to tell that was him. Hopefully no one else had been able to identify him.

"And it was smart of you to spend most of your time at sea, away from the public eye. I see you were successful in your attempts to get some money back. Very successful, by the looks of it."

"Yeah, it's been the time of my life," Purdue said with a roll of his eyes. "What the hell do you want? Come to check up on me?"

"Something like that," Sasha said. "I don't like you, Purdue. You know that. But I hate Julian, and he's only gotten worse since he got rid of you."

"Attempted to get rid of me," Purdue added quietly.

"He's worn your defeat like a badge. The leader of the Black Sun who finally got rid of their greatest enemy. It's been nauseating honestly. Hopefully it'll be worth it when I see his face, when he finds out you're still kicking."

"He can't," Purdue said. "Not yet. I'm not ready."

"I know," Sasha said. "I just came to tell you that your friends, Dr. Gould and Jean-Luc Gerard are still alive. They haven't given up yet either. Their guards managed to stop an escape attempt concocted by Dr. Gould. They almost got out themselves. But now ... now they've been put somewhere they definitely won't. It's all up to you."

"Isn't it always?" Purdue asked, feeling relieved to hear that his friends were at least still breathing. "Anything else you'd like to say to me while you're here."

"Just to hurry," Sasha said. "Julian is beginning preparations for the final phase of his plan."

"Final phase? The hell does that mean?"

"No one knows for certain," Sasha said, looking dour. "Scary isn't it? But whatever it is ... and knowing Julian ... it won't be anything good. You need to hurry so you can stop it."

"Why don't you do it then, aye? You can get closer to him than I could. Take him out and take over that damn order for yourself. Since that's obviously what you really want, isn't it?"

Sasha ignored his accusation, which probably meant it was true. "Despite what you would think, Julian has a lot of support from the others. He's almost beloved as a leader. Mostly, I think people just wanted to see things change. They mistake any change for being progress ... but Julian is destroying the Black Sun. If more people could see that, maybe then I would move against him. Maybe. As it stands now, I would be practically committing suicide if I tried anything."

"So you'd rather I die trying instead," Purdue said with a laugh.

"You're already dead, remember? That's why. But, I do have something that might be able to help you."

"And what's that?"

Sasha smiled and poked her head out the door. She said something and when she returned back into the room, a man was following her. Purdue recognized him immediately and couldn't believe his own eyes.

It was Sam Cleave.

Sam entered the penthouse behind Sasha and when he saw Purdue, his mouth fell open and his eyes grew wide with disbelief. He tried to speak but fumbled his own words, taking a step back and pointing at Purdue.

"You..." Sam tried to catch his own breath, still not believing what he was seeing. "She said you were alive, but honestly, I didn't believe a damn thing she said. You're supposed to be dead. Like dead-dead."

"Aye," Purdue said. "I still am, really, if you believe it."

"I ... I don't..." Sam grew flustered and even a little angry. "I honestly still don't believe I had two Black Sun operatives tell me all about how you died. It was all over the news. The house fire. Sasha said she dragged you out."

"The bastards did burn it to the ground, aye," Purdue said. "But yes, apparently ... well, I had a sociopathic guardian angel looking out for me. Sasha must secretly be in love with me. She stepped in and gave me a second chance at life."

"You don't make a lot of sense, you know that?" Sam said, turning to Sasha. "First you try to kill all of us for the Spear of Destiny. Then you save Purdue from a fire that your boss started. And you even got me away from your friends. The hell is your story?"

"I know how much you love a story, Sam, but as you saw on the way here, I'm not in the mood to share," Sasha said. "And that's all you need to know. My actions have already spoken for me."

"So you've been alive this whole damn time..." Sam turned his confused ire on Purdue. "The whole world thinks you died. Hell, I thought you died until sixty seconds ago, and you can't even bother giving me a phone call? Son of a bitch, do you have any idea how alone I was out there? Running all over the place trying to keep away from the Black Sun? You couldn't even give me the peace of mind to know that you were still out there somewhere?!"

"I couldn't," Purdue said, and honestly he did feel quite guilty about the whole thing. "I'm sorry, Sam, but it was too dangerous. I had to let everyone think I was dead. I had to essentially even be dead. Even now, David Purdue as he was is just ashes back in a burned house. I couldn't afford the order finding out that they failed. It's the only way I'll be able to hit them back, when they think I'm no longer a threat to them at all. It was the only way, I swear. It was the only choice that I could make."

"So you got play dead man while they hunted me day and night. Hardly seems fair, does it?"

"I know, Sam," Purdue said sympathetically. "But here we are. You made it. You know the truth now. I had nothing after they came after me, Sam. Nothing. They took all of my money. They took all of the artifacts. They took my home. They took Charles. They took Nina. They had everything. I just got back from a venture that has replenished some of my funds. Not all of it, obviously, but enough to start planning how we're going to get back at the order for this."

Sam didn't look enthusiastic about the prospect. If he wasn't exaggerating, then the fight with the Black Sun had already been raging for him, and he hadn't been faring too well in the battle. He probably wasn't looking forward to having to throw himself back at them anytime soon.

"They have Nina," Purdue reiterated. "We can't leave her behind. We have to get her back. We have to take it all back from them. Get rid of the Order of the Black Sun for good."

Slowly, Sam nodded. He walked up to Purdue and the two embraced in a rare hug between them. As much uncertainty and friction as there was, it felt good to be with a friend again; to know that there was someone reliable on your team.

"We'll get her back," Sam said. "We're going to get her back."

Sasha moved toward the door. "Now that you're both

reacquainted, I have to get back. Just remember what I said, Purdue. You need to hurry before it's too late."

"See you around then?"

Sasha stopped at the door. "No. No, I expect you won't see me again for some time. Probably not until you are hopefully standing over Julian's corpse."

Purdue folded his arms. "Looking forward to it."

The door of the penthouse closed and Purdue stood in mutual silence with Sam. Both men had gone through so much just to stay alive in the past few days. There was a whole war raging ahead of them, and both of them weren't fully prepared for it.

He turned back toward the ocean, with now even more stress on his mind. Whatever Julian and the Order of the Black Sun were concocting, it was coming, and there was now a doomsday clock looming over him. He already wanted to get his life back soon. Now he had to even sooner than that.

The power he needed to do that apparently rested at the bottom of the sea—so that was where they would go.

The End

Manufactured by Amazon.ca
Bolton, ON

32658122R00140